Fog on the Tolbiac Bridge

Léo Malet was born in Montpellier in 1909. He had no formal education and began as a cabaret singer at 'La Vache enragée' in Montmartre in 1925. He became an anarchist and contributed to various magazines: *L'Insurgé, Journal de l'Homme aux sandales* . . . He had various jobs: office worker, ghost writer, manager of a fashion magazine, cinema extra, newspaper seller . . .

From 1930 to 1940 he belonged to the Surrealist Group and was a close friend of André Breton, René Magritte and Yves Tanguy. During that time he published several collections of poetry.

In 1943, inspired by the American writers Raymond Chandler and Dashiel Hammett, he created Nestor Burma, the Parisian private detective whose first mystery, *120 Rue de la Gare* was an instant success and marked the beginning of a new era in French detective fiction.

More than sixty novels were to follow over the next twenty years. Léo Malet won the 'Grand Prix de l'humour noir' in 1958 for his series 'Les nouveaux mystères de Paris', each of which is set in a different *arrondissement*. *Fog on the Tolbiac Bridge*, depicting the 13th *arrondisement*, was first published in 1956, under the title *Brouillard au pont de Tolbiac*.

Léo Malet lives in Châtillon, just south of Paris.

GW00544537

Other books by Léo Malet in Pan

120 rue de la Gare
The Rats of Montsouris
Mission to Marseilles
Dynamite versus QED
Sunrise behind the Louvre
Mayhem in the Marais

Léo Malet

Fog on the Tolbiac Bridge

translated from the French by Barbara Bray
general editor: Barbara Bray

Pan Books
London, Sydney and Auckland

First published in France 1956 by Robert Laffont, Paris

Published in France 1983 by Editions Fleuve Noir as *Brouillard au pont de Tolbiac*

This edition published 1993 by Pan Books Ltd
a division of Pan Macmillan Publishers Limited
Cavaye Place London SW10 9PG
and Basingstoke

Associated companies throughout the world

ISBN 0 330 32745 3

9 8 7 6 5 4 3 1 (1 3 5 7 9 8 6 4 2)

A CIP catalogue record for this book is available from
the British Library

Phototypeset by Intype, London
Printed in England by Clays Ltd, St Ives plc

Contents

Léo Malet: an appreciation by Derek Raymond 9

1 Comrade Burma! 11
2 The dead man 22
3 1927 – the Vegan Centre and the anarchists 31
4 Information received 39
5 The Passage des Hautes-Formes 50
6 Belita 67
7 The stranger 76
8 The wandering corpse 83
9 The corpse reveals its secret 89
10 Friends 102
11 Burial-ground 113
12 From the viaduc d'Austerlitz to the pont de Tolbiac 131

1 Louvre
2 Bourse
3 Temple
4 Hôtel-de-Ville
5 Panthéon
6 Luxembourg
7 Palais-Bourbon
8 Elysée
9 Opéra
10 Entrepôt
11 Popincourt
12 Reuilly
13 Gobelins
14 Observatoire
15 Grenelle/Vaugirard
16 Passy/Auteuil
17 Batignolles-Monceau
18 Butte-Montmartre

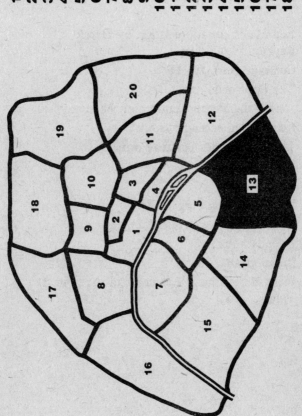

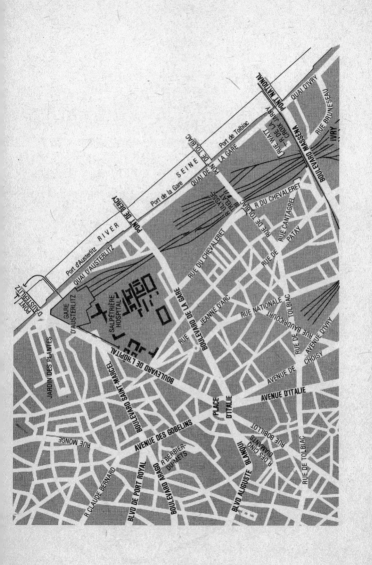

Leo Malet: An Appreciation by Derek Raymond

I feel very flattered, as a foreign writer, at being asked to give an appreciation of Léo Malet's work. To my mind, he is a writer whose books, if they had never been written at all, would have left a serious gap in French life as it had to be undergone during difficult and dangerous times – for there is nothing else quite like his work, transmitting, as it does, the sense of wartime France as experienced by ordinary people in terms of hardship and immediate menace rather than through the intellectual approach as expressed by Sartre or Camus.

He is one of the few living European authors who understands what the life of a fugitive, a hunted suspect, is really like; he must know what it is like, because he knows just how to describe it. He did this in the first book of his that I ever read, *120, rue de la Gare*, which to me remains among his very best. From the terror of running along empty nightlit streets, from the keen dread that tunes hearing up to the last bearable notch, from the intense need to start running sparked off by hearing a footfall the blind side of a rain-soaked street corner, from the justified paranoia of a man on the run who has just found that the door of the safe address he has been given has been nailed shut, Nestor Burma – Léo's major central character, who is surely immortal – is protected from the worst of all this by the author's own wry, rasping sense of humour – an apparent throwing away at the reader of some catastrophic situation which actually conceals a very real courage.

Like every writer who has mastered a genre, Léo has a passion for it – a passion generated, it seems to me, by his having lived both through the events he describes and extracted the essential from them – in Léo's case a precarious street existence in France during the Vichy régime. The measure of his mastery is that, without any waste, this passion is immediately conveyed to the reader. Writers, particularly in Europe, who have achieved that goal in this most difficult area of literary activity, the true thriller, are extremely rare, but for my money Léo is one of them.

It has from time to time been fashionable both for people who, no matter how much they have read, have no true feeling for literary creation and for others who really ought to know better, to dismiss this writer's remarkable oeuvre as 'pulp', and as superficial. What such critics have in my view quite failed to grasp is precisely what lies under their noses: that Léo's typewriter has rapped out what 'pulp' really is – for even if we can none of us define what that elusive word means, we realize instantly that we are face to face with it as soon as we start reading Léo, just as surely as we would if it were Chandler or Goodis.

And that is the main thing.

London, November 1991.

1 Comrade Burma!

My car was being serviced, so I took the Métro.

No doubt a taxi would be along in due course, but so would Christmas, and I didn't feel like waiting six weeks. Besides, it was drizzling, and there wasn't a cab to be seen. They shrink to nothing in the wet – that's the only possible explanation. Even when it stops raining they never want to go in the direction you're aiming at. Don't ask me why. The cabbies will tell you soon enough.

So I took the Métro.

I didn't exactly know why, but I was on my way to the Salpêtrière Hospital. My curiosity had been aroused by a mysterious letter that had reached my office in the rue des Petits-Champs by the midday post. I read it over yet again as the train made its way along the line that runs from the Eglise de Pantin to the Place d'Italie.

'Dear comrade,' said the note.

'I'm writing to you despite the fact that you're a cop now. You're a special kind of cop, and besides, I knew you when you were only a lad . . .'

The letter was signed 'Abel Benoit'. Abel Benoit? I

couldn't remember knowing anyone of that name either in my youth or since, though I did have an idea about the kind of background my billet-doux might have come from. It went on:

'There's a bastard up to no good. Come and see me in the Salpêtrière, Ward 10, bed . . .'

Here the scrawl became almost illegible. The number might have been either fifteen or four.

'. . . and I'll tell you how to get some friends out of a tight corner. Yours fraternally, Abel Benoit.'

No date, apart from a postmark showing the note had been mailed in the boulevard Masséna. The signature was quite firm, as signatures usually are, but the rest of the writing was pretty shaky. Nothing surprising about that: you don't go into hospital because you're in perfect health, and knees don't make a very good desk. The paper was the cheap stuff you can buy a few sheets at a time from any newsagent, and the envelope, which had been addressed in another hand, looked as it had been hanging around for some time in somebody's pocket or handbag. The whiff of cheap scent it gave off suggested the 'somebody' in question might be a nurse who relapsed into carelessness when she wasn't on duty.

At this point I put the letter away in my pocket. Why waste time theorizing about its meaning when I'd soon be talking to its author? Unless . . . Unless . . .

It suddenly struck me I might be the victim of a hoax. Abel . . . What if the 'bastard' turned out to be called Cain, and the whole thing was nothing but an April Fool's joke perpetrated in the middle of November?

Oh well, I'd find out before long. Meanwhile, even

dupes have a right to distraction. I was in a first-class compartment: there should be a decent pair of silken legs around somewhere, daringly crossed, to take my mind off the mystery. But it wasn't my day. I spied a fluffy-haired blonde at the other end of the compartment, but she was sitting with her back to me. All the other passengers were men: I wasn't interested in *their* legs. And their faces, on the whole, were unappealing.

Take the two young dolts opposite. They were got up in painfully stiff collars, like counter-jumpers in their Sunday best, and kept nudging one another, grimacing and giggling, as they gazed through the glass partition into the second-class section of the carriage. Perhaps they were going to the Salpêtrière too: it did have a ward for the mentally afflicted. A pity Professor Charcot had snuffed it in 1893: he'd have snapped them up for his researches.

I stood up.

I did so for various reasons. The yobs were getting on my nerves; I wanted to find out what it was they were so interested in; I was going to get out at the next stop; and I had a strange feeling, which I wanted to shake off, that someone's eyes were fixed on my back. I sauntered over and glanced into the more democratic part of the train.

The girl who was sending my two louts into ecstasies was standing up against the partition. She looked miles away in her own thoughts, but when her eyes met mine they gave an almost imperceptible flutter and then gazed straight back at me.

She couldn't have been more than about twenty or so, and was of medium height and well proportioned.

Her trench-coat, rather grubby-looking like all trench-coats, was open, revealing a red felt skirt nipped in at a slim waist with a studded leather belt, and a black sweater outlining a small but shapely bosom. Her shoulder-length blue-black hair framed a pretty, slightly swarthy oval face. She had big dark eyes and a sensual mouth enhanced with light red lipstick. Two large gold rings dangled from each of her ears, vibrating with the movement of the train. She looked like a gipsy, and had the stately bearing of most young women of her race. They're all, in a way, of royal blood.

A whole world of poetry, mystery and strange tradition lay between her and the two yokels. But anyone would have found her well worth looking at: I remembered having noticed her myself a little while ago, on the platform when I changed trains at République. What could this further encounter mean? Did I look as if I'd fall for having my fortune told?

The train rattled straight through the Arsénal station without stopping – it had been shut ever since the war – and eventually emerged from underground to cross the iron viaduct over the Seine. I stood with my pipe in one hand and my pouch in the other, watching the scenery go by, but still conscious of the gipsy girl's stare. The river looked leaden, and from it there rose a mist that boded no good. A freighter flying the British flag was moored by the Austerlitz bank; its stocky crewmen could be seen going about their work in the chilly drizzle. Further away, by the pont de Bercy, a crane revolved on its base like a model on a catwalk presenting a gown.

As I finished filling my pipe the train drew up with

a screech of brakes, and I found myself looking down from the Métro on to the smoky vista of the main-line Austerlitz station. As I got out I was assailed by one clammy blast of air from the river and another from the main-line terminal below. Both draughts sent litter swirling along the platform. The two youths didn't alight, but they'd have to seek some other diversion now, for the girl had left the train at the same time as I did and was now walking along in front of me. She still might be following me – some tailing *is* done that way. But somehow I didn't think she was a fellow gumshoe.

Completely ignoring the attention she attracted, she made her way through the other people on the platform to the map of the Métro adorning the wall. She moved gracefully, like a dancer, hips swaying, skirt swirling out from beneath her coat and brushing against a pair of small, flat-heeled but elegant brown leather boots.

She appeared to be studying the map. Another train came in on the opposite platform, stopped to set down and take on passengers, and drew out again. I could feel the vibrations it set up through the soles of my shoes. A phone rang in the station-master's office. I lit my pipe.

We were the only people left on the platform. Most of the other people who'd alighted were no doubt hurrying to see their nearest and dearest in the Salpêtrière. The porter whose job it was to water the floor and incidentally douse the customers' feet hadn't yet come on duty.

I walked over towards the girl.

She must still have been keeping an eye on me,

because when I was only a couple of feet away she turned and spoke.

'You're Nestor Burma, aren't you?'

'Yes. Who are you?'

'Don't go,' she said, by way of reply. 'Don't go. There's no point.'

Her voice was as voluptuous as her mouth. Slightly husky, and rather tired-sounding, with a tinge of melancholy. There was sadness, too, as well as a hint of fear, in those great gold-flecked brown eyes.

'Don't go where?' I asked.

'Where you're going . . .'

She lowered her voice.

'. . . To see Abel Benoit. There's no point.'

The wind blew a lock of hair in her face, and as she tossed back the mass of black tresses her gold earrings jangled and I could smell the same cheap scent as I'd noticed before on the letter.

'No point?' I said. 'Why not?'

She swallowed painfully, drew a deep breath that showed off her breasts to advantage, and murmured a phrase I'd heard very often in the course of my career. The words were almost inaudible, but I didn't need to hear them.

'He's dead,' she said.

I didn't answer at first. The warning clang of baggage trolleys rose from the main-line station below.

'So it wasn't a hoax!' I said.

She gave me a reproachful look.

'What do you mean?'

'Nothing. Go on.'

'That's all.'

I shook my head.

'No. You've said either too much or not enough. When did he die?'

'This morning. He wanted to see you, but he didn't have time . . . I . . .'

She swallowed again.

'I ought to have posted his letter sooner.'

She put her hand into her coat pocket – that limbo where so many urgent messages are trapped – and got out a crumpled packet of Gauloises. But she put it away without taking out a cigarette. I realized I'd let my pipe go out, and put that away too.

'So it was you who posted the letter?'

'Yes.'

'And if I'm not mistaken you've been following me ever since I left my office?'

'Yes.'

'Why?'

'I don't know.'

'Perhaps to make sure I was going to do as I was asked?'

'Perhaps.'

'Hmm . . .'

A man came up the stairs on to the platform and started pacing up and down, watching us out of the corner of his eye.

'So we've been travelling together ever since I took the Métro at the Bourse. If you knew he was dead, why didn't you tell me before?'

'I don't know.'

'You don't seem to know very much, do you?'

'I know he's dead.'

'Was he a relative of yours?'

'A friend. An old friend. A kind of adoptive father.'

'What did he want with me?'

'I don't know.'

'But he spoke to you about me?'

'Yes.'

'How?'

She brightened up.

'When he gave me the letter he said you were a cop, but not an ordinary cop. You were a good chap and I could trust you.'

'And do you?'

'I don't know.'

We had been here before. I raised an eyebrow. She shrugged.

'He's dead,' she said again.

'So you say.'

She stared.

'Don't you believe me?'

'Listen, young woman . . . Have you got a name, by the way?'

Her red lips trembled into almost a smile.

'You're a cop all right,' she said.

'I don't know . . . Hey, I'm starting to talk like you! We ought to get on well together! . . . What's wrong with asking your name? Abel Benoit told you mine, didn't he?'

'My name's Belita,' she said. 'Belita Morales.'

'Well, Belita, my motto is seeing's believing. What if Abel Benoit, instead of being your friend or adoptive father or whatever, was someone another person didn't want me to see, despite or even because of the fact that *he*, Abel Benoit, wanted to see *me*? Do you get my meaning? . . . I turn up, you say he's kicked the bucket, and I just go away again. Unfortunately I'm not like that. I'm very persistent.'

'I know.'

'Oh, so you do know something?'

'Yes. He told me . . . Oh, all right, if you don't believe me, go on in and see for yourself whether . . . whether he's really dead. But I don't want to set foot in there again . . . I'll wait for you outside.'

'Oh no!' said I. 'We need to have a little talk, you and I, and I don't want to lose you. You're coming with me.'

'No, I'm not.'

'What if I make you?'

I doubted whether I could but it was worth a try.

Her eyes flashed.

'I wouldn't attempt it if I were you!'

By now the platform was full of people waiting for a train, and we were beginning to attract attention. The onlookers probably thought I was just another fool of a victim about to be gulled. They mightn't be far wrong.

'OK,' I said. 'I'll go in on my own. But don't think you've seen the last of me!'

'Of course not! I shall be waiting for you.'

'Where?'

'Outside the hospital.'

'Oh yeah?'

'I'll be waiting for you,' she repeated curtly, as if angry that anyone should doubt her word.

I turned on my heel and went down the stairs and along the corridors leading to the exit. Out on the boulevard de l'Hôpital, I looked back towards the entrance to the Métro station.

Belita Morales, if that really was her name, was walking slowly after me, her hands in her pockets, her pretty little face held defiantly up to the rain. With every step I took the distance between us grew.

The last nurse I'd come across had been called Jane Russell. I can't recall the name of the film, but in it Jane Russell cured everybody except the audience. They were left distinctly feverish. But the nurse I met in the Salpêtrière, in the corridor leading to Ward 10, was quite a different proposition. A cure for love; flat back and front. I started to tell her who I was looking for . . .

'Smoking's forbidden,' she barked, pointing at my pipe.

'But it's not even lit!'

She sniffed, pursing thin pale lips. I told her again I was there to see Abel Benoit, bed 15 or 4, I wasn't sure which. She asked me to wait a moment, nodded me over to an uncomfortable chair, and disappeared into a glass-walled office. I sat down and waited, sucking on my empty pipe. A faint hum of voices rose from the visitors in the adjoining ward. A little old woman shuffled past, dabbing at her eyes with a handkerchief. The frosted glass of the office showed nothing of its occupants but an occasional vague outline. After some aeons the nurse came out again. About time. I couldn't have lasted out much longer, breathing in that horrible hospital pot-pourri of ether, antiseptic, drugs and doomed humanity.

'Abel Benoit, you said? Are you a member of the family?'

I stood up.

'A friend.'

'He's dead,' she said, with as much expression as a vat of tetrachloride.

The words were as familiar to her as they were to me.

I smiled.

'Did you have to look it up in a ledger?' I asked.

She looked more frigid than before, if possible.

'He died this morning. I didn't come on duty till midday.'

I scratched my ear.

'That's funny.'

'What is?'

'Nothing. Where's the body?'

'In the morgue. Would you like to see it?' She sounded like a hooker inviting me up to her room.

'If I may.'

Dead or alive, this stranger who seemed to know me interested me strangely.

'Come with me, then,' said the nurse, unbending slightly, collecting a big blue cape off a hook, and leading the way downstairs. We went through a court-yard and past a chapel, then along a path bordered with busts of famous quacks. No one else in sight. Then out of the drizzle there appeared a well-built figure in a greenish raincoat and a grey trilby, coming towards us hand outstretched and wearing a mocking smile. I can't say I was surprised. It was Inspector Fabre. A henchman of Superintendent Florimond Faroux, head of the Paris CID.

'Well, well, well,' he said. 'If it isn't Comrade Burma!'

2 The dead man

I returned his handshake, then his hand.

'Good thing I'm not a cop,' I said. 'I'd have to report you to your superiors for using that sort of language. What's up? Have you joined a Communist cell?'

'I ought to be asking you that,' he said.

'I'm not a Communist.'

'You used to be an anarchist. Perhaps you still are. And there's nothing to choose between them as far as I'm concerned.'

'It's a long time since I threw any bombs,' I sighed. 'But don't forget what Clemenceau said: "Anyone who isn't an anarchist when he's sixteen is a fool." '

'But didn't he also say that anyone who's still an anarchist when he's forty is just as bad?'

These pleasantries looked like going on for some time. The nurse cleared her throat pointedly. Fabre thanked her for her help and sent her away. Then he turned to me.

'I suppose you came here to see Abel Benoit?'

'And I suppose you expected me to?'

'More or less. Come with me.'

And he started to walk towards a small outbuilding made of brick.

'After you with the explanations,' I said. 'Judging by your attitude the case doesn't seem very serious. Except for the deceased, of course.'

'Just an ordinary case of assault as far as we can tell so far. The fact that the victim's snuffed it doesn't make any difference. Nor does the fact that he knew you – but that did strike us as amusing, Superintendent Faroux and me.'

'So you decided to look into the case more closely – is that it? And set a sort of trap?'

'Just routine, old man. I assure you I was only here by chance. But I don't regret our meeting. Anything for a laugh.'

'What's funnier still is that I *didn't* know Abel Benoit from Adam.'

'Why were you asking to see him, then?'

'Because he wrote and asked me to come.'

'*He* knew *you*, then?'

'Perhaps.'

'No perhaps about it. He wrote to you. And he kept track of you professionally.'

'Did he indeed!'

'We found a whole stack of press cuttings about you and your cases at his place.'

'Really?'

'Yes.'

'That doesn't mean anything. I've got a drawerful of cuttings about Marilyn Monroe.'

'He wrote to you.'

'How do you know I haven't written to Marilyn? . . . Ah well, I don't want to contradict a corpse. I suppose we must have met at some time or other. But when and where? . . . Just a minute . . . Oh, I see! He was an anarchist – is that it? He moved in the same circles as I did in my misspent youth?'

'Exactly! You can be quite quick when you want to. Have you got his letter on you?'

'I left it in my office,' I lied.

'What did it say?'

'Nothing much,' I lied again. 'He called me dear comrade, said he'd like to see me even though I was a cop, and gave me his address here. In the hospital, not the morgue.'

'Hmm . . . I suppose his mind was affected. By age and his injuries.'

'Was he so old?'

'He wasn't young. Sixty-one. You start getting a bit frail at that age. And being attacked must have undermined his principles. He wanted to get his own back on his attackers – he must have known who they were – and instead of contacting us, the real police, as he ought to have done, he meant to ask you to punish them. That's how I see it. What about you?'

I shrugged.

'I don't know. I've only just heard about it.'

'Right. Do you still want to see him?'

'Might as well, while I'm at it! There mayn't be much point now, but I like to be able to put a face to a name . . . Abel Benoit – it still doesn't ring a bell.'

'He did use other names too.'

I'd already thought of this possibility.

We were now entering the morgue. A gloomy-looking attendant in a grey overall stubbed out an illicit fag when he saw us and assumed a blasé expression.

'Visitors for number 18!' Fabre sang out blithely.

Yet another alias for the party in question.

The attendant led us down to a medium-sized room with lights suspended from the ceiling on chromium rods. Then he strolled casually over to a sort of ice-box and drew out a trolley. Upon it, under a sheet, lay a motionless shape. One of the wheels of the trolley grated against the concrete floor. I remembered hearing perambulators make the same sound. The wheel had come full circle, from the cradle to the grave. The attendant moved the trolley under a lamp, switched it on and looked at us to see if we were ready, then deftly twitched back the sheet. The inspector reached out a hand to stop him revealing more than the face.

'I know my job!' the man protested.

'And I know mine!' rejoined Fabre.

Me too! He wasn't just trying to spare my feelings. There must have been something on the body, a tattoo mark perhaps, a sign that might have put me on the right track sooner than the cops would have liked.

The dead man looked about sixty: bald, with a white Marshal Pétain moustache and a hooked nose that was slightly crooked. Though his face was now ashen, gaunt and grim, he must once have been quite good-looking. Especially twenty or thirty years ago.

'Well, Burma?' said the inspector.

'Well, when I knew him – *if* I knew him – he had more hair on his head and less on his upper lip. And he probably looked more cheerful.'

'He looks pretty livid now.'

'Maybe he doesn't like the cold.'

We fell silent. Then:

'Might as well go,' I said. 'I never saw him before. Unless . . .'

'Unless what?'

'I don't know . . . That hooter . . .'

I bent down closer to the corpse and moved around the trolley to look at the dead man's face from the other side.

'He's got two profiles,' I observed.

'A left and a right. Just like everyone else.'

'No – *not* like everyone else. The crooked nose makes him look different according to the point of view. Very useful for giving cops the slip.'

'And have you ever known someone like that?'

'I can't quite remember . . . Anyway, the name Abel Benoit still doesn't mean anything to me. But didn't you say he used different names? One for each profile, perhaps? Tell me some of them.'

'Lenantais was his real name. Albert Lenantais. And it wasn't a nickname, even though he *was* born in Nantes.'

'Good God!'

I didn't feel like any more backchat now. The name took me back more than a quarter of a century.

'An old acquaintance,' I said slowly.

'The nose is probably the only thing about him that's still the same,' said the inspector. 'Funny. Any plastic surgeon could have straightened it out for him.'

'I don't suppose he wanted to look like Martine Carol or Juliette Gréco. He was an eccentric.'

'Tell me what you know about him.'

'What can I say? He was a good sort. A good friend. A shoemaker by trade, so everyone called him the Cobbler.'

'Yes, that's on his file . . . Are you're sure it's him, then?'

I looked again at that face, so severe in death. I forgot the moustache and summoned up a mop of tousled anarchist locks. That and the nose were enough.

'Quite sure,' I said.

'Thank you.'

'For what? The fingerprints must have put you in the picture already. But what about that?'

I pointed to the torso concealed by the sheet.

'Isn't there a tattoo mark on his chest? *That* would have told me who he was straight away. But I suppose letting me see it would have been too easy! . . . The way you cops waste tax-payers' money!'

'Do you remember what the tattoo mark was of?'

'There were two. A coin on his arm, and the words "Neither God nor Master" on his chest.'

'Quite right.'

And Fabre, taking hold of the sheet, turned it back to reveal the torso. The image of a French coin, complete with the symbolic female Sower, was intact on one arm. But the G of 'God', on the chest, had been effaced by a stab wound, and the word 'Master' was underlined by another deep slash.

'The anarchist motto. Not very original,' said Fabre.

'Very stupid,' I said. 'I told him so at the time, even though I was years younger than he was.'

'I thought you approved of those sentiments?'

'I disapproved of tattooing. Still do,' I said, starting to pull the sheet up over the corpse's indecently bald head. The attendant took over, with a meticulous, almost maternal gesture.

'The reason I mentioned fingerprints,' I went on, 'was that Lenantais used to be a bit of a subversive, and before I knew him he'd been mixed up in some counterfeiting racket. Hence the picture of the coin.'

'Yes. He got two years for that.'

'He was keeping his crooked nose clean when I met him. But though he never tried to convert anyone else to subversive ideas, you got the feeling he'd probably get on the wrong side of the law again himself. I could never understand why he went in for those tattoos – it's easy enough for the cops to identify old lags without providing them with clues.'

My youthful sagacity seemed to amaze both my companions.

'Had your head screwed on the right way even in those days, didn't you?' observed Fabre. 'Tell me – where was it you met Lenantais?'

'That's another funny thing. It was quite near here. At the Vegan Centre in the rue de Tolbiac . . . We both lived there for a while . . . He didn't get very far in those thirty years, did he?'

'We know he didn't smoke or drink or eat meat. Was he actually one of those Vegan nuts?'

'No – a nut of a different kind. I'll give you an example. He was absolutely down and out – there were days when he didn't have anything to eat – but before he fell on hard times he'd been made treasurer of some small group—'

'So he helped himself from the till?'

'No, that's just what he didn't do! There were a

couple of hundred francs in the coffers – which was a fair sum in those days . . . around 1928 – and the lads thought they'd seen the last of their cash, though they didn't like to mention it in the circumstances. But the money belonged to the organization, to his friends, and Lenantais, even though he often went hungry, never touched it. That's the sort of man he was when I knew him.'

'An honest crook!' said Fabre sarcastically.

'A man like anyone else. People are all alike, whatever their opinions. Neither all good nor all bad. As you, with your experience as a cop, ought to know.'

'Well, I call him a nut! You've always mixed with nuts, as far as I can see!'

'Does that include my friend Florimond Faroux, your boss?' I asked.

'Do I hear someone taking my name in vain?' said a voice.

I turned round to see the chief of the Paris CID holding out his hand.

'So now the big chief goes out of his way for an ordinary case of assault, does he?' I said.

'Yes, when he finds out Nestor Burma knows the victim! The nurse on Ward 10 told Fabre a chap with a bull's-head pipe was asking after Abel Benoit, and Fabre phoned and told me. We already knew Benoit was interested in Burma. So here we are!'

He turned inquiringly to Fabre.

'I don't think we'll have any trouble with him this time,' said the inspector. 'He didn't identify the body straight away—'

'I hadn't seen the man for donkey's years!'

'—but when he did he told me all he knew. I've been watching him closely, and I don't think he's shamming!'

Faroux looked at me.

'When was it you last saw Lenantais?'

'1928 or '9.'

'And since then?'

'Nothing.'

'Why did you come to see him? Did you read what had happened to him in the papers?'

'Was it in the papers?'

'I don't know. Maybe a couple of lines in a piece about muggings by foreigners . . .'

'Lenantais wrote to him,' said Fabre.

Faroux asked to see the letter. I made the same excuse as I had to Fabre.

'Why don't you tell me what this is all about?' I said. 'All I know so far is that Lenantais kept press cuttings about me, and that you think he was stabbed by some North Africans. Come on – give!'

Faroux looked around.

'All right,' he said. 'I don't suppose this is a case where you can show us up, and you might have some useful ideas. But let's go somewhere more cheerful.'

3 1927 – the Vegan Centre and the anarchists

The huge window made the dormitory look rather like an artist's studio, and the dress of some of the inmates reinforced that impression. These impecunious anars and economic drop-outs went in for velvet jackets, corduroy trousers, wide-brimmed hats and floppy ties. And lived by shifts that weren't always entirely legal.

The upper part of the window panes was clear, but the lower half had been covered in white paint so that when the inmates undressed they wouldn't offend the sight of virtuous citizens living on the opposite side of the street. Someone's claustrophobia had got the better of him, though, and he'd scratched enough of the paint away to show, as through a fog, what was going on in the rue de Tolbiac outside.

Not that there was much to see. The youth standing there now with his face pressed to the glass couldn't understand why anyone had gone to the trouble – and risked the wrath of the puritanical theosophists who allowed them to sleep in the Centre for fifteen francs a week – to reveal such an unprepossessing scene.

A few scrawny acacia trees cringed against gusts laden with snow; the worn pavement was covered with slush as *far as the eye could see. But the youth was looking out at the gloomy prospect with a certain amount of interest. A man in his shirtsleeves, with black curly hair, came up and peered over his shoulder.*

'Mal tiempo,' *he growled, then swore and went back to his bunk. He'd been sleeping for most of the past three days, too depressed to make any effort.*

The boy glanced at an alarm-clock that hung from a string over a heap of tousled blankets. Three in the afternoon of Tuesday, 15 December 1927. In ten days it would be Christmas. He felt a slight pang.

Albert Lenantais, sitting on a stool near the stove with a pamphlet in his hand, turned his blue eyes towards the window, then stood up and came over.

'What was that the Castilian said?' *he asked the youth.*

'Lousy weather.'

Lenantais brought his crooked nose close to the glass.

'Yes . . . It must be better in the south, eh?'

'Mmm . . .'

'Aren't you fed up with Paris?'

'I don't think I'll ever be fed up with it. I haven't been very happy here so far, but—'

'I know how you feel . . . Some people have had enough of it, though.'

'When I have, I'll go home.'

'Yes. You can do that, at your age. Have you got enough money for the journey?'

'I'll hop a train.'

Lenantais shrugged and went back to his stool, and the youth soon returned to his bunk. Lying there with his hands clasped behind his head he could keep an eye on the alarm-clock. At four o'clock it would be time to go to work. That blasted snow! If it came down like yesterday

*it would be no joke trying to sell newspapers. But he had
to eat. He mustn't let himself go, like the Spaniard . . .*
Albert Lenantais seemed to disapprove of his idea of
travelling without a ticket. Yet if what people said was
true, the Cobbler had done two years in jail for being
involved in counterfeiting. The boy started to wonder
about him. But no – you didn't ask questions among the
anarchists. He looked down the row of beds. At the other
end of the room three men were eagerly discussing some
socio-biological problem. Nearer, a dreamy young man
lay on his bed, quietly smoking a long-stemmed pipe. He
was known as the Poet, though no one had seen any of
his verses. The Spaniard was tossing and turning under
his blankets. His neighbour snored beneath a poster
announcing a meeting of the Rebels' Club that evening at
the union headquarters in the boulevard Auguste-Blanqui.
The subject to be debated was 'Who is guilty? Society or
the Lawbreaker?' and the speaker was André Colomer.
The snorer had spent the previous night illegally sticking
up posters to advertise this gathering. Operating in a tem-
perature ten degrees below zero and with nothing but a
glass of milk to keep him going, he'd torn off the corner
of each poster, where the administrative stamps should
have been, in case he was nabbed by the police. The cops
were supposed to think the stamps had been stolen by
street urchins. His equipment – a bucket and a brush –
stood at the head of his bed, beside an empty haversack
and a box full of newspapers.

The door at the far end of the room opened, admitting
a smell of vegetables from the kitchen downstairs and a
young man of about twenty with his right hand covered
in an enormous bandage. The newcomer grunted a general
'Hallo', dropped on to a bed not far from that of the

youth who'd been looking out of the window, unwrapped the bandage and wiggled his numbed fingers. They showed no sign of any injury.

'Have to fake them up a bit!' the new arrival muttered to himself. His eyes were unpleasantly dull. He wore a small brown moustache and a lot of smelly hair-cream. 'Those quacks and their rotten check-ups!'

He took a notebook out of his pocket and started doing his accounts. The youth yawned, stood up, and got an armful of unsold newspapers out from under his mattress, sorting them into two piles with Paris-Soir on one side and L'Intransigeant on the other.

'Still serving out the middle-class press, then?' said the man with the bandage, disagreeably.

'That's the third time you've asked me the same question,' answered the youth. 'The first time I thought you were joking, and laughed. The second time I said I had to eat. And now I say go to hell!'

'And he calls himself an anarchist!' sneered the other. 'The only bomb he knows is a bombe glacée!'

'Let him alone, Lacorre,' said Lenantais from where he was sitting, not even looking up from his pamphlet. 'What do you expect him to do? And do you think you're a better anarchist than he is?'

His voice was cold and cutting.

'Yes, I do,' replied Lacorre.

Lenantais put down his pamphlet.

'I doubt if you know the meaning of the word,' he said. 'It's all very well to come along one fine day and say "I'm one of you" . . . That's easy. We let people come and go as they like. We don't cross-examine them.'

'I should think not!'

'But you're not my idea of an anarchist.'

'What is your idea, then?'

'I don't propose to waste my time explaining.'

'An anarchist has some sense of his own dignity!' cried Lacorre. 'He isn't passive and resigned, like this kid – he wouldn't stoop to selling those bourgeois rags. An anarchist sticks up for himself, he gets by, he steals . . .'

'Does he indeed!'

'Yes!'

'Rubbish! It's up to everyone to manage as best he can, so long as he doesn't impinge on anyone else's freedom. The boy sells papers. You fake injuries. Everyone's free to choose.'

'Listen to the anti-law brigade!'

Lenantais jumped up, his crooked nose quivering.

'Leave them out of it! Fakes who sweat blood at the thought of a medical check-up would do better to keep quiet on the subject until they've held up a bank messenger or two! I've met too many loudmouths like you, full of fine theories, but nowhere to be seen when other poor fools translate their principles into action and get nabbed for their pains.'

'Poor fools like Soudy and Callemin and Garnier . . .' said Lacorre.

Lenantais cut him short.

'They've paid the price and I respect them. If you knew what you were talking about, and how far they're above such wretches as you, you wouldn't insult them by uttering their names!'

Lacorre was crimson with fury.

'I suppose you have robbed a bank?' he cried.

'I've paid the price too. I've served two years in jail for counterfeiting – anyone'll tell you that. I'm not proud *of it, but I reckon it's a cut above faking accidents!'*

'I haven't finished yet!' growled Lacorre. 'One of these days I'll get the bit between my teeth and polish off a bank messenger myself!'

'I don't doubt it!' said the other. 'You're quite capable of a clever wheeze like that! And when you've killed one of the idiots who cart other people's fortunes about in return for a crust, you'll go to the guillotine and have your head cut off before you've had time to buy yourself a new hat for it out of the proceeds! Personally, I don't think it's worth it. The best thing—' Here he began to laugh. 'I'm seriously contemplating it! The best thing would be to attack a bank messenger without doing him any harm, and not be found out, and just live in peace on one's ill-gotten gains – if gains are ever anything else!...Of course, it's easier said than done.'

Lacorre looked at him pityingly.

'And you accuse me of talking rubbish? God, you give me a pain, the lot of you!'

As he flung out, slamming the door, Lenantais laughed quietly and went and switched on the lights. A few anaemic bulbs shed a sparse yellow light through the huge room. Lenantais sat down again by the stove. The long-haired debaters went on talking, too interested in their own discussion to have taken any notice of the latest flare-up between Lacorre and Lenantais. The Poet went on smoking his pipe. The youth did some sums in his head. The Spaniard and the bill-sticker slept.

Perhaps it was that day, perhaps another, that a thin man with a mop of hair and a beard came into the dormitory. He used a gnarled stick as a kind of staff, and wore leather sandals and no socks.

'Is Comrade Dubois here?' he asked.

Then he sniffed.

'It stinks in here,' he said. 'Stinks of . . .'

He stopped: he'd spotted the Poet smoking. And darting across the room he snatched the pipe out of the young man's mouth and dashed it to pieces against the wall.

Amid general protests, Lenantais spoke.

'Comrade Garone, you have acted in an authoritarian manner unworthy of an anarchist. Would you like to force the rest of us to follow your example and go down on all fours to browse for our food? You're quite at liberty to preach against tobacco if you please – I don't smoke myself, as a matter of fact – but you must win people over by argument, not by force . . .'

This gave rise to a lively argument.

The lad who'd looked out of the window took the Métro in the Place d'Italie and went over to the rue du Croissant in the second arrondissement – the newspaper district. Here he bought a few evening papers which he came back and sold in the 13th arrondissement, round about the Vegan Centre. At eight o'clock he counted up his meagre takings, put the unsold newspapers away under his bed, and made his weary way to the meeting of the Rebels' Club in the boulevard Auguste-Blanqui. Here he found Albert Lenantais and a couple more kindred spirits from among the Parisian anarchists. One, a twenty-year-old, was discreetly known only as Jean: he was absent without leave from the army, and might be picked up at any moment by the military police. The other, slightly older, was called Camille Bernis. Both were quiet and polite, taking no interest in other people's affairs and keeping themselves to themselves; but they looked very determined, and an occasional flash of fanaticism came into their eyes. They didn't live in the Centre, but they went back there with

Lenantais and the youth after the meeting. All four sat up into the small hours discussing the pros and cons of illegal action, perched on a bed amid the wailings of the December wind, and lit only by an oil lamp too small to disturb the sleepers all around them. Lenantais's contributions were very vague. Perhaps he was musing on some grand Utopian project like the one he'd spoken of to Lacorre.

Faroux's voice seemed to reach me through a layer of fog.

'Come on, Burma – let's be off . . . Hey, what's the matter? You look very strange!'

I pulled myself together.

'I was thinking about my youth. I'd never have believed it was so far away.'

4 Information received

Once outside, I filled and lit my pipe. Faroux had driven to the hospital in an unmarked car, and the driver waiting beside it, who seemed to have spent his time watching the trains go by on the overhead Métro line, was in plain clothes. But despite all the camouflage it was plain this was a police matter.

The gipsy girl had promised to wait . . .

I gave a furtive look round. No red skirt in sight. I'd been away some time now, and the early dusk was made dimmer by the thickening fog. Still, it wasn't so dark I couldn't have spotted Belita if she was still there. She just hadn't waited. Perhaps she'd never meant to. Or more probably she'd been scared away by the arrival of the police contingent. Her people could smell a cop a mile off.

The driver got into the car, behind the wheel, Fabre beside him. Faroux and I sat together in the back.

'Where shall we go to talk, Burma?' asked Faroux. 'You're the expert on bars.'

'Well, since I can't get away from the past, what about the Rozès in the Place d'Italie? I seem to remember their croissants used to be very good.'

'Place d'Italie, Jules!' Faroux told the driver. 'Burma's hungry!'

'No, I'm not,' I said as the car nosed between the pillars supporting the Métro and out into the boulevard de l'Hôpital. 'I mentioned the croissants because I remembered how in my vegan days I used to eat three or four at the counter there. And when I paid I said I'd only had one!'

'Why are you telling me that? Isn't your reputation bad enough already?'

'It's profitable to have a bad reputation these days. Mine's still too good by half! And I like the idea of going back to the scene of my crimes with a gaggle of cops.'

'It was all such a long time ago,' said Faroux.

'You mean it comes under the statute of limitations?'

'Croissants may, but crooks are making a mistake if they assume real crimes do. We never entirely close a case, and many a villain finds himself caught out at last, years after the event. And do you know why? Because a cop can get tough when he's thwarted, especially when he has to put up with cracks about efficiency from the public. He broods. He's always on the look-out for a clue. The thing becomes a personal vendetta.'

'Like with old Ballin, you mean,' said Fabre.

'Yes,' answered Faroux. 'That's funny – it was supposed to have happened around here, the case that eventually sent him off the rails . . . A clerk carrying a lot of money vanished without trace near the pont de Tolbiac in 1936 . . . Ballin worked like a slave on the affair without ever getting anywhere, and it preyed on his mind so much he became unbalanced and couldn't concentrate on anything else. He was still worrying away at it when the war started. In 1941 the Germans sent him to a concentration camp, and he came back completely all-in. Mad as a meat-axe. He's been retired for a long time now, but they say he's still looking for a clue . . .'

Faroux was supplying more juicy examples of the local past when we reached the Place d'Italie. He said he was trying to cheer me up: he could see I was affected by Lenantais's death.

'It's not so much his death,' I said, 'as coming across him again after all this time.'

'Same thing.'

'I suppose so . . . It's like a sort of loss . . . What a district, eh? I wonder if I'll ever see it with the sun shining?'

The square was gradually being infiltrated by fog. The tyres of the passing traffic hissed on the wet road. The cafés had all switched on their lights; a neon sign twinkled over the glassed-in terrace of the Brasserie Rozès. We parked as close as we could, and Jules, the driver, went and waited for us at the counter (perhaps to keep an eye on the croissants), while Faroux, Fabre and I settled down in the corner furthest from the door. The bar itself was crowded and noisy, but the only other seated customers were a couple of lovers with eyes only for each other. Someone was playing a pinball machine. Someone else selected a Georges Brassens record from a juke-box.

When the waiter had brought our drinks – an apéritif for me, a Vichy water for the inspector, and a steaming grog for the superintendent – Faroux spoke.

'A bit irregular, discussing a case in a place like

this,' he said. 'But Burma seemed to need a drink, and I don't think this Lenantais business will turn out to be anything but an ordinary assault . . . Whatever ideas he may have had in the past, and whatever his record, Lenantais had kept out of harm's way for years. He didn't mix with any political or philosophical groups, and he'd managed to start a little business. And what do you reckon it was, Burma?'

'Well, he was a first-class shoemaker . . .' I said. 'Did he set up on his own?'

'No, that wasn't it. Perhaps he couldn't afford to rent decent premises . . . Though he did have a shop of sorts . . .'

'More like a shed,' said Fabre.

'Yes,' said his boss. 'In a dreary little alley called the Passage des Hautes-Formes, between the rue Nationale and the rue Baudricourt – just off the rue de Tolbiac. It's not really a cul-de-sac, but it's marked as one, so it doesn't attract customers. But Lenantais wasn't the kind to *want* customers – too much like employers . . . And he certainly wouldn't have worked for anybody else . . . We know he did make a pair of shoes from time to time, but guess what he really earned his living from?'

'No idea.'

'Junk! He was a rag-and-bone man! He bought and sold second-hand clothes and furniture, and with that, and the odd bit of cobbling, he managed to provide for his needs – and to be his own master. In short, in his own way he solved the great problem of existence. Did you get a look at his clothes, back there in the hospital?'

'No.'

'Well, they were of very good quality. Not the height of elegance, mind you, but not the kind of thing most junk merchants wear.'

I began to wonder . . .

'No,' said Faroux, guessing at my thoughts, 'I don't think he was a fence . . . We keep tabs on *them*, and if he'd dabbled in that sort of thing we'd have found out . . . So now we come to his final misadventure.'

He threw away his cigarette stub and finished off his grog.

'Three nights ago he was set upon in the street – by a couple of North Africans, according to him, who stabbed him a couple of times and stole his wallet. He managed to drag himself home and appealed for help to a neighbour. A sort of gipsy girl.'

'A sort of something,' said Fabre sardonically.

'Whoever she is, she lives in a shack next door to Lenantais's place. I'd say he was too old to have slept with her, though you never can tell with these free-thinkers.'

'Sixty isn't as old as all that,' I said, thinking of my own distant future and Sacha Guitry's recent past.

'I wasn't talking about physical ability,' laughed Faroux. 'I was referring to the difference in their ages. She's only twenty-two and he was nearly forty years older . . . Anyhow, after the attack he was too badly hurt for her to be able to do anything for him.'

'I thought gipsy women had secret remedies up their sleeves!'

'Not this one, apparently. She's a modern gipsy, who's broken with her tribe and probably with all their hocus-pocus too . . . So she got Lenantais into the old van he used for his work and drove him to

the Salpêtrière. The people there notified the local
cops of what had happened, of course—'

'Just a minute,' I interrupted. 'Why did she take
him to the Salpêtrière? Isn't there a hospital closer to
where he lived?'

'Yes – the Lannelongue. But she drove him to the
Salpêtrière. She didn't say why – I suppose it was the
first one she thought of . . . Anyhow, our colleagues
on the spot, who like to keep an eye on the North
Africans, went to have a look at where their latest
victim lived. At first they thought the fight might have
been a settling of political scores – that neighbourhood
is full of Arabs, some friendly enough with the French
and some not. But Abel Benoit – from the papers in
his pockets they still thought that was his name – was
a bit of a puzzle. For one thing, there were those
subversive tattoo marks. And then among the stuff at
his place they found a lot of anarchist literature dating
back to '37 and '38 – the Spanish War seems to have
put an end to his career as an activist. Finally there
was an up-to-date file on me.'

'You!'

'Indirectly! It contained press cuttings from the *Crépuscule* – articles by Marc Covet about your cases. Of
course my name was mentioned a few times. Well,
the local police had taken the wounded man's fingerprints right away, and they soon told us who he really
was. In 1920, under his real name, he'd been mixed
up in a counterfeiting racket; he was also known as
an ardent and dangerous anarchist.

'Well, Burma, I always take cases seriously when
your name comes into them. And what with the press
cuttings and the letter Lenantais sent you, I thought

44

you might have known him in the past. He seemed to be getting a bit better, and I was just going along to the hospital to ask him a few questions when I heard he'd suddenly kicked the bucket. The rest you know. What do you make of it?'

'Nothing!' I said. 'All right, I did know Lenantais once, but so long ago we'd become practically strangers . . . We're not sitting here cudgelling our brains about a simple case of mugging, are we?'

'Simple? Not when he took the trouble to send you that letter, and in those circumstances. Why did he drag *you* into it?'

'He was still a bit of an anarchist,' Fabre suggested. 'And although he wanted revenge he couldn't bring himself to call in the police.'

'Maybe,' said Faroux doubtfully. 'If he'd written to the President of the Republic I wouldn't have minded. But to Burma! . . . That makes me smell a rat.'

'Well, I'm sorry my name has that effect on you. You must try to struggle against it. But I'm afraid I can't help you – all I know I've found out from you.'

Faroux was still sceptical, but I eventually headed him and his followers off, agreeing I'd send them Lenantais's letter. After declining a lift and seeing them safely on course for the Quai des Orfèvres, I went back into the brasserie and phoned Marc Covet at the *Crèpuscule*.

'I want you to do me a favour,' I told him when I'd finally got past a dumb blonde and a chap who sounded as if he was breaking in a new set of false teeth. 'Dig out the chap who covers small news items in the 13th arrondissement and see what he has on a character called Abel Benoit – real name Lenantais –

who got himself stabbed and robbed by some Arabs a few days ago. Then work it up into an article and see it gets into the paper.'

'Is this the start of something?' he said eagerly.

'No, the finish of the person in question. He snuffed it. It was someone I used to know ages ago.'

'And you want to give him some posthumous publicity?'

'No. He wouldn't have liked appearing in the papers. He was a modest sort.'

'And this is how you respect his wishes?'

'Maybe.'

I hung up. The phone booth was next to the cloakrooms. In the gents' I read Lenantais's letter one last time, then tore it in small pieces and pulled the chain on it. If Faroux wanted to know what was in it he'd have to use a diving bell now. I had another drink at the bar, went into a nearby shop and bought a map, and set out down the avenue d'Italie.

It was almost dark now, with a slight mist wreathing everything. Cold droplets lurked on every twig and at the edge of every awning, ready to fall on passers-by as they hurried along, their heads bowed as if in shame. Here and there between the street lamps a café threw out on to the pavement a swathe of warmth and light, a whiff of alcohol, a jangle of jukebox music.

Walking past with my pipe in my mouth and my hands in my pockets, safe from the elements in my sheepskin jacket, I felt a strange pleasure tinged with a certain unease: in streets I'd once trailed through on my uppers I now strode comfortably along on thick-soled waterproof shoes. True, I was often hard up even now, but there was no comparison between that and what I'd gone through in the old days. I'd made some progress . . . But so had everyone. In one direction or another! . . . Why the devil did Lenantais have to go and drag me back into the past?

When I reached the rue de Tolbiac I took the 62 bus going towards Vincennes and alighted at the next stop, near the Passage des Hautes-Formes. The ill-lit, narrow street, paved with ancient flagstones, bulged up in the middle and sloped down on either side to a gutter full of water, no doubt the product of the residents' ablutions. An alley cat, disturbed by my attempts to negotiate the uneven surface, streaked across in front of me and vanished into a ruined hovel. The other houses were modest, not to say humble, dwellings built on at the most two floors, some facing directly on the street, the rest set back beyond a garden or, more precisely, a yard. Somewhere a radio was blasting away and a kid was doing its best to drown it. These were the only sounds, apart from the distant hum of the traffic in the rue de Tolbiac. I spotted two wooden doors standing side by side and leading to two identical shacks. The first was fearsomely bolted and barred, and on it, painted in black, was the legend: *Laguet. Rags and bones.* But I doubted whether Lenantais could have been Laguet as well as Benoit. However, the second door was marked: *Benoit. Rags and bones. Junk.* The locks didn't look too difficult here, and the police hadn't bothered to seal the place up. But I didn't want to waste my time, or risk attracting attention, by trying to get in. I could come back and nose round Lenantais's place some other time if necessary. I'd really come here to find the gipsy girl who was supposed to live next door.

I tottered a little way further. Beyond a crumbling wall surmounted by rusty railings, and across a tiny courtyard, I could just make out through the haze a little one-storey cottage. A light winked in an upstairs window. The gate hardly creaked at all when I pushed it open, and I had no trouble crossing the yard and getting into the house. I was met with a smell of decaying flowers, the funereal odour of dead chrysanthemums. Looking round, I saw that a ladder did duty as a staircase, its upper end disappearing through a trap-door in a corner of the ceiling. A shaft of light flooding down from the aperture fell on a number of wooden boxes lying at the foot of the ladder, together with a flower-seller's big wicker basket.

I didn't need to strain my ears to tell that there was somebody upstairs. A voice was bawling out a string of furious oaths. I crept to the foot of the ladder. A heavy footstep sounded overhead. The shouting had stopped . . . Then came a dull thud, rather like a shot, followed by a stifled groan.

I froze.

The imprecations started up again. Then there was another thud. But that wasn't a shot! My lips twisted in disgust. A gun would have been cleaner and less cruel. I shinned up the ladder and peered into the upper room.

At first an enormous fanny entirely blocked my view. Here was someone who wasn't too bothered about her figure. Then I made out a huge pair of shapeless legs looming there in white cotton stockings that didn't match, while their monstrous owner stood with arms akimbo, puffing and panting like a steam engine in the intervals of screaming curses. She was holding a very nasty-looking whip.

The room was small and poorly furnished, but clean. Belita Morales was crouching in one corner, her legs drawn up under her red skirt, her face contorted with pain, her eyes flashing with helpless hatred. She wasn't wearing her trench-coat now, and her sweater was torn. Some bloody weals marred her magnificent bosom, but her breasts stood up as proudly as ever, as if defying their tormentor.

5 The Passage des Hautes-Formes

I leapt up the last rungs of the ladder and into the room.

'Oh?' I yelled. 'We torture little girls, do we?'

The frightful old bag whirled round with surprising agility, and the air she displaced didn't smell of Chanel No. 5 . . . Nor was her front view any improvement on the back. Great boobs stuffed into a grimy blouse; no neck; a moth-eaten fur jacket slung over massive shoulders; a wrinkled, swarthy, toothless face adorned by a single eye. Whether as the result of a fight or through the pox, the left lid was permanently closed. Greasy black locks reminiscent of the Gorgon completed the picture.

'What is it?'

Her voice sounded like someone scraping a saucepan.

'Only me! The genie out of the bottle! I always arrive in the nick of time! . . . Hallo, Belita!' I gave her a friendly wave.

' "Belita!" ' sneered the woman. She turned to the girl: 'I suppose he's the one you sleep with! . . . Answer, Isabelita – you slut!'

The girl's answer was a weary gesture.

'I don't sleep with anyone,' I said. I was about to let her have a few oaths of my own when she raised her arm. I just had time to jump aside as the thong of the whip snaked towards my face, and the blow fell harmlessly on my sheepskin jacket. I staggered a bit, but managed to clutch the thong and jerk the handle of the whip out of the old witch's hand, dragging her down on top of me as I hit the floor, with her weapon safely if uncomfortably underneath me. God, I thought her hundred kilos would smother me! Fate was always inventing new ways to lay me low – was I going to be asphyxiated, this time, by an enormous pair of knockers? An epic struggle ensued, with the woman thumping me all over and calling me and my respectable parents all the names she could lay her tongue to, while I squirmed like a fish, trying to get out of the way. I couldn't end the fight by dotting her on the head with my gun: it was out of reach in my back trouser pocket. Just as I was about to apply a solution from a more accessible pocket, Belita intervened, springing on my adversary and dragging her off by the hair. But I still thought it worthwhile chucking a handful of tobacco dust into the female Cyclops' eye, and while she buried her head in her hands, howling with pain, I snatched up the whip and gave her a taste of her own medicine. I was so furious I really think I might have killed her if she hadn't, in her own elegant lingo, begged for mercy.

'Get your great boobs out of here and never let me set eyes on your lousy carcase again!' I replied, careful to match her refinement. 'I could have you arrested if I chose! But I don't like the cops any more than you do!' (Nor did I want to answer their questions.) 'Go on – scram!'

She whined some more, rubbing her eye and groping for the whip. I was still holding it. I gave it a crack. She jumped as if she'd actually felt it.

'I'm keeping this as a souvenir,' I said. 'Clear out!'

She tumbled down the ladder as best she could. I didn't do anything to help her. If she smashed her face in, so much the better. But she got to the bottom all right and vanished into the darkness, spitting out a few farewell objurgations.

I went down too to make sure she'd really gone. Then I shut the door, which she'd left open, bolting it as well in case she changed her mind and came back. I didn't actually regret what I'd done, but I wasn't very glad I'd had to do it. The old horror probably belonged to a local gang, and it wouldn't be long before they were on my track. I got out my gun, checked it, stowed it in a handier pocket than before, and climbed up the ladder again.

The room was just an attic, but the girl had made it quite pleasant to live in. The wooden floor was scrupulously clean, as were the main items of furniture: a deal dresser and a low bed. I had no means of telling if the latter was comfortable or not, but it was covered neatly by a check cretonne spread. There was a rudimentary wardrobe in one corner, and in another a few kitchen utensils and a plastic bowl and jug. No dirty plates or smeared glasses. On the dresser, beside a vase of flowers that were beginning to droop, two cigarette ends in an ashtray advertising an apéritif. A cheap mirror hung on the wall. A little stove gave off an agreeable warmth, and the whole scene was lit by a wall-lamp – a curved metal bracket fitted with a large electric light bulb. Nothing sordid. Poor but honest.

'So here we are!' I said to Belita.

She was sitting on the bed. She hadn't tidied herself up: with a kind of innocent shamelessness she'd left her injured bosom as visible as ever. She sighed, then tossed back her hair in what looked like a habitual gesture, making her earrings jangle.

'Thank you,' she said, looking up at me. She had a voluptuous-sounding voice. 'But you shouldn't have . . .'

'I've no regrets,' I said. 'Except perhaps about the tobacco dust – I don't like stooping to be a bastard to another bastard. It should be possible to win without that. As Abel Benoit taught you, I expect?'

'Yes.'

'We'll come back to him later . . . But why didn't you wait for me?'

'I saw the cops arrive.'

'That's what I thought. Right . . . We'll talk about that later. But for the moment we must see to those . . .'

I moved over to inspect her injuries. The weals inflicted by the whip looked nasty, but they weren't so serious as I'd expected. This didn't make the old woman's savagery any better. The girl gave a sudden shudder.

'I . . . I'll see to it,' she said.

'A few cold compresses should do the trick,' I said.

'Yes.'

I turned and went over to the window. Outside, the fog had grown thicker. The whole dreary alley was shrouded in it. I took out my pipe and started to fill it. But my fingers were shaking and I felt ill at ease. Perhaps it was the nauseating smell of the flowers rotting away downstairs. I could hear Belita moving about behind me, opening the dresser, moving a saucepan. I lit up.

'What are those flowers doing downstairs?' I asked.

'I sell them.'

'In that state? You wouldn't have many customers.'

'I let everything drop after Benoit went into hospital.'

'So you're keeping the flowers to make chrysan- themum jam?'

'Oh, they can be thrown away now.'

'Good!'

I went down the ladder, grabbed up the basket and the boxes and slung the whole lot out into the yard.

'So here we are!' I said again, back in the upper room.

Belita had put on a short-sleeved blouse. The neck was discreetly low.

'I feel a bit better now,' I said. 'What about you?'

'I'm all right. You're very kind.'

I sat down on the bed and held out my left palm.

'Look and see if you're right!'

She drew back.

'I don't know how to do that sort of thing,' she said.

'I do.'

I took her hand and pretended to study it.

'Abel Benoit, whom you call your adoptive father, was your neighbour long enough to rid you of a lot of false ideas, including racial prejudice. He helped you emerge from the tribe and become a free individual – if there is such a thing as freedom. Very praiseworthy. But at the same time he destroyed a lot of local colour and made you forget how to tell fortunes.'

She smiled.

'There's some truth in what you say.'

'Perhaps all is not lost, then. Come on, have a try – see if you can remember the secrets of your race.'

She sat down beside me, took my hand, and gravely started to study it. Her hair brushed against my nose.

'Well?'

She pushed me away.

'Nothing. I can't read hands . . . I don't know . . .'

Her eyes showed a flicker of fear.

She stood up.

'But I trust you . . .' she said, and disappeared through the trap-door. When she came back she was carrying an old wallet which she laid down on the bed. I stared at it.

'It's his,' she told me. 'He said he'd been attacked by Arabs, but it's not true. He told me to hide the wallet to make everyone think he'd been robbed. But he hadn't.'

'I suspected as much,' I said.

But when I examined the wallet, all I found was thirty thousand francs in five-thousand-franc notes. No clues.

'Excuse me,' I asked, 'but is this all?'

She was angry and hurt.

'What do you take me for?' she said.

'There, there – don't be cross. I'm very kind and you trust me, but I have to ask some questions – it's my job . . . I'll hang on to the wallet. You may have hidden it very well, but it'll be even safer with me. From the police, I mean . . . But here—' holding out the money – 'I think you should have this.'

'I don't want it,' she said.

'Don't be silly. Benoit doesn't need it any more, and *I* don't want to treat him like an ordinary client. Are you going to take the lolly or not? No? Right – I'll look after it, but it's yours whenever you need it.'

I put the wallet away in my pocket.

'I'm afraid we've got to have a long talk. What about going out for something to eat first? My treat.'

'We could eat here,' she said, 'if . . .'

'All right. Thanks. This place is nice and warm . . .'

Lenantais's teaching had borne fruit. Or rather vegetables. That's all there was. And no wine. Personally I could have done with a nice thick steak and a bottle of vino, but once wouldn't kill me. Belita got a folding table out from behind the dresser, fetched a couple of stools from downstairs, then set about getting the dinner. I sat on the bed smoking my pipe, watching her swish around in her felt skirt and wondering what the hell I'd got myself into.

'Hope you don't mind my smoking?' I said, just for something to say. I felt ridiculous.

'I smoke myself sometimes. Benoit didn't, and he said I ought not to either. But he left me free to choose.'

'You weren't even born when I knew him. He was a good chap then.'

'He didn't change . . . It's ready,' she said.

It wasn't as bad as I expected. As we ate she talked to me about Lenantais.

★

She'd always known my quixotic friend as Abel
Benoit. He'd met her four years before. His rag-and-
bone business had taken him to a patch of waste
ground at Ivry, beyond the Pont National, where she
lived with some distant relatives: she was an orphan.
For some reason or other she was being bullied by
the fat floozy I'd just sent packing, and Lenantais had
intervened. He was a strong, bold fellow who seemed
undiminished by time. He'd stood up to the gipsies
and advised the girl to leave them. She didn't do so
right away, but one day when she couldn't stand the
situation any longer she legged it over to the old
anarchist's place, and he undertook her education. He
taught her to read and write, and to reject the prejudices of her race. The little shack next door to his
was to let, so he fixed it up for her to live in. It was
his idea that she should be a flower-seller, and she'd
lived happily ever after . . . until three days ago.

'Hold on a minute,' I said. 'Didn't the gipsies ever
try to get you back, or at least to take their revenge?'

'No.'

'So they've abandoned their traditions too, have
they?'

'They've decided to make the best of a bad job . . .
I think.'

'What do you mean?'

Her pretty face became impassive.

'Nothing.'

'It's a good thing you trust me, isn't it!'

She hesitated for a moment. Then:

'Well . . . I've seen Benoit talking to Dolores two
or three times . . . Dolores is the old woman you saw
just now . . . And with Salvador, one of our young

men. He's a rough customer and doesn't mind using a knife, but he's too bright to make trouble if he can avoid it . . . At least, I think so. Well, before you arrived Dolores told me Benoit had made a bargain with them, and I'm sure she wasn't lying . . .'

'A bargain?'

Her eyes filled with tears.

'He bought me. Paid them to leave me alone. He worked like a slave to do it. I was worth more to them like that than if I'd stayed.'

'Another lost illusion!' I lamented. 'Even gipsies will do anything for money nowadays! Ah well, it takes all sorts . . . And I suppose that was really the best solution . . . ?'

'There was only one thing they'd never have forgiven him.'

'What was that?'

'If he'd slept with me.'

'And . . . ?'

'He never laid a finger on me. And they must have known it, or there'd have been trouble. They knew we were just comrades. We feel some things instinctively, you know.'

' "We"?'

'In some ways I'm still one of them.'

'I suppose that's what Dolores thinks,' I said. 'I imagine she heard somehow that the old boy couldn't pay up any more, and she came to get you back?'

'Yes.'

Hmmm . . . Lenantais read Nietzsche, but it was Dolores who followed his doctrine and came after the girl with a whip.

I looked at Belita in silence. I didn't think much of

her chances. I couldn't always be there to protect her.

'Let's get back to our friend,' I said. 'You were saying that three nights ago . . .'

She told me what she'd already told the cops and what Faroux had passed on to me, but added some details that were new. Lenantais had been seriously injured and she thought he was going to die in her arms. She tried to do something for him, but soon realized she couldn't cope. When she talked about taking him to hospital he jibbed. No, no, out of the question. But finally, when he saw how upset she was, he agreed.

' "I'll go to the Salpêtrière, then," he said. "Just drop me there and don't say anything. My private affairs are my own concern. I'm a bit the worse for wear, but I'll get over it." He said that just to reassure me. "If the cops poke their noses in I'll spin them a yarn." '

'What it he who chose the hospital?'

'Yes.'

'Did he say why?'

'I got the impression he knew a doctor there.'

'Did he mention his name?'

No. He'd been too busy telling Belita to take his wallet and hide it. And if anyone asked questions she was to say the same as he would: that he'd been mugged and robbed by some Arabs. That's all the cops needed to know. Then he fainted. She wondered how he'd lasted that long. Then she'd got out his van and driven him to the Salpêtrière.

'I didn't care about the consequences – I mean about the police and what they might think. All I wanted was to get him properly looked after. To save his life. I knew he couldn't have done anything wrong. I'd known him for four years – I'd had plenty of time to learn how good and open and generous he was.'

She clasped one of my hands in hers. Her bosom heaved; there was a curious light in her brown eyes.

'He taught me . . . tried to teach me . . . that revenge is wrong. But I belong to a race that doesn't forgive! Maybe it's one of my old prejudices, but I can't help it – Benoit was so good to me I can't just do nothing! I want the swine who killed him to pay for it with his own blood, drop by drop!' Her vehemence made her more beautiful than ever. 'You'll avenge him, won't you? You *will* avenge him? I'll help you!'

'How?'

'I don't know. But I'll do whatever you tell me!'

'Calm down, my dear,' I said. 'The only way to avenge him without betraying his own beliefs is to prevent the person he mentioned in his letter – the person who killed him, no doubt – from carrying out his designs. But unfortunately I can't perform miracles. I don't mind having a go, but I do need some sort of a clue . . . The murderer couldn't be one of your lot, could he? – that Salvador, or some other gipsy? Because unless Lenantais's wits were astray when he wrote to me, the words he used couldn't have been meant to refer to one of them. Did he look to you as if he was still all there when he gave you the note?'

'Absolutely. And he thought he was out of danger, though he did say there was no time to be lost.'

'He didn't go into detail?'

'No.'

'Let's go back a bit. You drove him to the hospital. What happened then?'

She'd told the people at the Salpêtrière the truth, more or less, including the patient's name and address. They hadn't kept her, and she'd gone back to the Passage des Hautes-Formes. The next day the police, tipped off by the hospital, came and searched Lenantais's place and questioned Belita about him, but not too aggressively. They'd even said she could go and see him.

'It was then that he gave me the letter,' she said. 'He'd written it secretly. And as he didn't have an envelope . . .'

'You got one and addressed it for him.'

'Yes. He told me to look you up in the phone book.'

'Is that all? Didn't he say anything else? Try to remember. It could be very important. Sometimes the smallest thing can trigger me off.'

I felt about as optimistic as I did about winning the next National Lottery, for which I hadn't got a ticket. Belita frowned and pondered.

'He said he was feeling better and would soon be coming out of hospital, but that time was passing and he must act fast. He said the police had found out he was once an anarchist and so would be keeping an eye on him. He mentioned you and said you were a good chap and I mustn't be put off by your profession . . .'

'Is that all?'

'Yes.'

'But I'm a fool,' she said. Her sad face grew even sadder. 'A fool, if not worse. For the very first time I didn't trust what he said.'

So she hadn't trusted me, either, and had put off

posting the letter. When she finally did so, yesterday evening, it was too late. Lenantais had suddenly got worse, and had died this morning, as they told her when she went to see him at the hospital. So then she'd thought that if I really had been his friend I'd be willing to avenge him. She learned from the post office what time the letter would be delivered, and hung about near my office in the hope of meeting me. She'd somehow managed to find out what I looked like.

'I saw you come out, and followed you. If you went straight to the cops, the real cops, I was going to give up. But if you did what Benoit had asked you, like a friend . . .'

'And I passed the test?'

She smiled back at me.

'Yes.'

'Unfortunately that doesn't get us anywhere. If only that note had mentioned a name!'

'He was in a hurry, and he didn't think he was dying . . .'

'Mm . . . Of course . . . Hey! They couldn't have finished him off in the hospital, could they?'

She had no answer to that.

We'd finished our frugal meal. As she made the coffee I got out my pipe. The problem could be summarized as follows: Lenantais was attacked by a stranger who intended to harm others too. Friends of Lenantais, and friends of mine, if I understood him correctly. I hadn't seen Lenantais since 1928 or 1929, so I must have lost sight of the friends in question at about that time. But if I was to make a list of all the people I'd known thirty years ago, and then try to get in touch with them, it would take me the rest of my life, and then some. The easiest solution was to assume Lenantais's mind had been wandering and the whole thing was meaningless . . . But fortunately or otherwise it seemed to me it did mean something.

'I must search his place,' I said. 'The police have searched it already, I know, but they were thinking about North Africans. And something that was irrelevant for them might be a vital clue for me.'

I got up and went over to the window. The Passage des Hautes-Formes no longer existed. The fog had swallowed it up.

'Visibility's down to a couple of yards. I can try to force the lock without being seen. Unless you've got a key . . .'

'No,' said Belita, coming over and standing beside me. I was aware both of the cheap scent she wore and of her own smell – that of a young animal. 'The cops took them all. But there's another way in besides the gate on the street. A little door leading off my yard.'

'Let's go!'

I put on my sheepskin jacket, she put on her trench-coat, and down we went. Out in the yard the fog, clinging round our shoulders like a wet sheet, engulfed both the vapour of our breath and the smoke from my pipe.

The ex-counterfeiter wasn't afraid of thieves – you had to grant him that. The little door had no lock on it. But it didn't open straight away when I lifted the latch. Something soft was blocking it.

I shuddered, and swore a silent oath. Could it

be . . . ? One dead man had addled my brain; perhaps another would clear it again. I gave the door another push. It still wouldn't open.

'Have you got a torch, Belita?'

'Yes. Upstairs.'

'Would you go and fetch it?'

After she'd gone I put my hand round the door and encountered what felt like a clammy bundle of rags. And that, as the torch soon revealed, was all it was. I can't remember if I was disappointed or not. I shoved the door as far open as I could, and we both entered the shed, stepping over a bundle of odds and ends of material that had fallen off a heap. Belita, who knew where the switch was, turned on the light. I'd never seen such a mess. I'd never find anything in all that chaos, I thought – always assuming there was anything to find. But what did I expect? A rag-and-bone man is a rag-and-bone man, and an anarchist's idea of order isn't likely to be the same as everyone else's. A prehistoric Ford van with battered paintwork stood in a space near the main door, but apart from that the place contained nothing but bundles of old papers, old clothes, old iron and discarded articles of furniture. It all lay about in indescribable confusion, its original, professional clutter made worse by the police: they're not in the habit of putting things back where they found them. I was very sorry to disappoint the gipsy girl – I could feel her looking at me, expecting some sort of miracle – but all I could do was stare.

'Did he sleep up there?' I asked, pointing to a spiral staircase leading to an upper floor.

'Yes.'

We climbed up the rickety stairs and were confronted by another mess, though this time, apparently, the chaos was due solely to the police. One wall was covered with bookshelves: their contents had been slung on the floor. All the anarchist and other subversive literature – pamphlets, newspapers and periodicals – that lay strewn around would no doubt have delighted the heart of a collector. But it didn't tell me anything. I opened a table drawer. The papers inside were of no interest. Part of the room was arranged as a cobbler's workshop. I went over to the bench. Tools, pieces of leather, work in progress. I shrugged.

'Let's get out of here,' I said. 'We're getting frozen stiff for nothing.'

So we went back next door.

'I could do with something hot, couldn't you?' I said.

'I'll make some more coffee.'

She started to fill the saucepan.

'Oh, I forgot to ask you . . . Where was he attacked? Did he tell you?'

'He mentioned the rue Watt – the street that goes under the railway, from the rue Cantagrel to the quai de la Gare.'

The rue Watt might be expected to shed a little light. But I wasn't going to count on it.

I spent the hours that followed interrogating the gipsy girl. First I made her tell me all she knew about Lenantais – his habits, his obsessions if any, the names of his business contacts. We both almost lost our voices in the process, but it left me none the wiser. I was tired. It would have been easy to chuck the whole thing. But Lenantais had been a good friend, and even though he was dead I couldn't let him down.

Then it was my turn to tell Belita what I knew about him. About the Lenantais I'd known in the past. It took some time, and I gradually came to talk about myself as well, or rather about a kid called Nestor Burma who was well and truly down and out in this part of Paris before she was born. Someone I'd forgotten all about until the day before. Someone I now remembered with indefinable feelings.

'It's a lousy district, this,' I said. 'And like a lot of other lousy districts, it's changed a good deal since my day . . . Got better in a way . . . But there's still an atmosphere about it . . . A sinister atmosphere. And in some places, some streets, you can't help breathing it in . . . Get out of it, Belita. Sell your flowers wherever you like, but don't stay here. It'll destroy you as it's destroyed others. It reeks of poverty and dirt and unhappiness . . .'

We were looking at one another, I sitting on a stool and she curled up on the bed. I saw her give a slight start.

'Hey, I've started to call you "tu"! I hope you don't mind? It's an old anarchist custom!'

'I like it.'

'Good. If you like, *you* can call *me* "tu" too!'

6 Belita

I put some wood on the stove and went and looked
out of the window to see if the Passage des Hautes-
Formes was still there. Yes. But the fog had gone.
And dawn was gradually revealing the shapes of the
houses opposite. I turned towards the bed. I couldn't
see Belita very clearly, but I could guess at the pretty,
wilful little face still slumbering amid the scattered
hair. Things, good or bad, move fast sometimes.

'*If you like, you* can call *me* "tu" too!'
   She didn't answer. Just lit a Gitane.
   I went on.
   'I had such a rotten time in this area I can't bring
myself to like it. Why did Lenantais have to go and
drag me back here? Couldn't he have gone and sold
his rags and bones somewhere else? . . . I'm in a nice
mood, aren't I? I'm not usually like this unless I'm
sloshed. And I'm certainly not sloshed on your hospi-
tality, am I, Belita?'
   'Certainly not!' she laughed.
   I got up and paced about for a bit, perhaps to make
sure I didn't stagger. I didn't stagger. But for some

reason or other I did feel drunk. A floorboard creaked as I trod on it, as if to mock me.

'I'll be better tomorrow . . . ,' I told Belita. 'I'm supposed to be able to K.O. any mystery. I must try to prove it to myself . . . Lenantais must have wanted to play a trick on me. He didn't like the idea of my becoming a cop, even a private one, so he arranged all this to pay me out! . . . Ah well, I'd better be off!'

I looked at my watch. The last Métro must have gone long ago, and there wasn't much chance of finding a taxi in this godforsaken quarter and this fog. It was nice and warm in here. The stove was purring cosily. Fancy having to go out and trudge through those lousy streets yet again!

'Stay,' said Belita softly.

And I suddenly remembered Dolores and her no doubt equally vindictive pals. Unless I was just looking for an excuse.

'I suppose it might be best,' I said with a laugh. 'If I caught a cold I wouldn't be as lucid as I'll need to be! And if Dolores comes back for her whip I'd like to give it to her myself . . . Right – pass me a blanket, Belita. I'll stretch out on the floor by the stove. You get some sleep too – you must be tired after tonight's session. How do you feel, by the way?'

'It's almost stopped hurting now.'

My comments during the next few minutes must have made Dolores' ears burn, the cruel old cow. Meanwhile Belita had taken a blanket off the bed and I'd rolled myself up in it, having first made up the stove and deposited my pipe within easy reach on the table. A proper little boy scout. Belita switched off the light. The stove hummed away comfortably in the dark; it was old and cracked, and threw quivering shafts of rosy light on to the walls and the floor.

'Here's something else that reminds me of the Vegan Centre,' I said, launching into an anecdote that had just occurred to me . . . With time and distance the story that followed had lost its sting and was only colourful and amusing – when told in well-lit, comfortable surroundings to an audience of cops or journalists or anyone else who had enough to eat. But here in the Passage des Hautes-Formes it sounded wretched and depressing, like the original experience. Why had I dug it up? Perhaps because I hadn't had a drink since that apéritif in the brasserie . . .

'Yes,' said Belita, when I'd finished.

She was in bed by now. The tip of her cigarette glowed in the dark like a beacon. Then she put it out.

'Goodnight.'

'Goodnight.'

You could almost feel the fog swirling round the house, trying to find a way in. The only sound was an occasional creak from one of the ancient rafters . . . After a while I heard the girl get up. Then she seemed to be fumbling about among the kitchen equipment.

'Anything wrong?'

'No.'

'Shall I switch the light on?'

'No, I can manage.'

She'd taken the lid off the stove to put some coal on. Her dressing-gown fell open as she bent over, and the glow from the fire lit up her bosom. She closed the stove again. There was a faint smell of coal.

'Are you looking to see if it's sunny?' I asked.

By now she'd moved over to the window.

'A real pea-souper!' she said.

I joined her. Yes, pea-soupers were the local special-ity. I tried to peer through the fog, but what was the use? I knew it was nasty, sooty and hostile. But inside the room it was very nice.

Very nice . . .

We were side by side now, conscious of one another's warmth and defying the elements. My hand brushed against her breast.

She drew back.

'No, you mustn't . . .' she murmured.

This was a lousy part of the world, where I'd been crushed and humiliated, never treated as a real human being . . . I took her in my arms, clasped her very tight, and started to kiss her. She tried to pull herself free . . . A lousy part of the world, and once again it was aiming to treat me as if I was still a helpless kid . . .

But I couldn't take my revenge through her . . . I let her go.

'Anyway, you're a gipsy,' I said.

Silence. A dull, stifling silence. A sudden spurt of flame in the stove briefly lit up the room.

'Oh,' she sighed. 'What does that matter . . . ?'

Then she put her arms round my neck and her lips on mine. Our hearts seemed to beat together. Nothing else existed. Even the fog had gone.

So there we were! Things, good or bad, sometimes happen fast. I'd found a cure for my complexes about the neighbourhood, anyhow. I felt like a new man. I was going to do great things! . . . Well, I was going to try. In reality I wasn't any further forward than I'd been the night before. But maybe something would turn up . . . I watched Belita as she awoke, stretching like a little cat. Chance hadn't treated me too badly so far. I went over to the bed.

'Don't say a word,' I murmured, stroking her hair. 'There's nothing we can do about it.'

She smiled.

'Who said I wanted to say anything?'

'You might have regrets . . .'

She didn't answer.

'Or you might want to say good morning!'

'Good morning!'

She took my left hand and ran her fingers over the palm.

'What does the future say?'

'You know I can't tell fortunes,' she said curtly, dropping my hand.

'Go on! Didn't you foresee that we were going to sleep together?'

'Perhaps.'

'Well then! . . . What else?'

'Nothing.'

Her face went blank. I tilted her chin and made her look at me.

'You saw something nasty was going to happen to me.'

She pulled away.

'Of course not. It's all nonsense.'

'Naturally. If it wasn't I'd take you on as my assistant and in next to no time you'd tell me what Lenantais's message meant. But even if despite what you say you do think there's something in fortune-telling, you needn't worry on my account. Brickbats aimed at

Nestor Burma rarely hit their target. I always give the lie to prophecy. If my horoscope promises me a windfall you can be sure I won't get a sou . . . What would you like for breakfast?'

'Anything.'

'I'll go and get some croissants.'

It was chilly out, but there wasn't going to be any fog, at least that morning. A yellow sun gilded the gaunt acacias in the rue de Tolbiac. People hurried about their business, cars whizzed by. It was a district like any other, with shops and bistros and paper-sellers. I bought the 5 a.m. edition of the *Crépu* from an old woman with a red nose and mittened fingers black with printer's ink. Marc Covet had obeyed my orders, and I went into a bar on the corner of the rue Nationale to read his article over a coffee and a sandwich. Covet had even bettered my instructions: it was quite a long piece, and dug up the counterfeiting affair that Lenantais had been involved in all those years ago. His recent attackers were described as North Africans. The paper gave his address and his real name, and mentioned that he was a reformed anarchist. Very good. Now all I had to do was wait for someone to read the article – or some other paper's version of it – and go into action . . . Yes, but who would that someone be, and what sort of action would *he* take?

I did my shopping and went back to the Passage des Hautes-Formes bearing croissants and a bottle of milk. Belita was in the yard, putting the dead flowers that I'd chucked away the night before into the dustbin. Her dressing-gown was more revealing than ever.

'This is no time to be catching cold,' I said, putting

the milk down and taking her hungrily in my arms. Just like a schoolboy! But she didn't seem very delighted. On the contrary, she tried to disengage herself, staring at something behind me. I turned round.

He was standing outside the gate, his hands in the pockets of a well-worn leather jacket: a young chap of about my own build, quite handsome if you like carnivorous beasts. He had piercing blue eyes, a swarthy skin and a curly moustache; a twisted smile revealed a set of pointed teeth. His trousers were blue and fell in concertina folds over almost new shoes. He wore a grubby hat tilted over one ear. The ear sported a gold ear-ring.

'Salvador, eh?' I breathed.

Belita only closed her eyes. Yesterday Dolores. Today Salvador. I took a step towards him.

'What do you want?' I asked.

He didn't move.

'Come on,' he said.

'Who – me?'

He looked daggers.

'Her,' he said. 'Isabelita. Ready, slut?'

'What's that – a password?'

'Eh?'

'What is it then?'

'You shut up! Come on, Isabelita!'

He still didn't move. Evidently the sort of chap who thought he only had to give his orders.

'Clear off before I make you!' I said.

'You and who else?' he sneered.

'My friend here,' I replied, taking out my gun and moving nearer.

'Beat it, Salvador!'

He hadn't expected the revolver. After he'd got over the surprise he stared at it as if he'd never seen a gun before. Or as if it impressed him about as much as a bar of chocolate.

'Bastard!' he muttered.

'Don't imagine I'm bluffing,' I told him. 'There aren't any witnesses. The first bullet's for your legs, the second will just be to warn you . . . I shan't tell you again . . .'

He was still starting at the gun.

'And no funny business, because you know I mean it . . .'

'I know.'

His lips quivered. He was thinking. It took him some time – I suppose he didn't do it very often. Finally he drew back.

'All right,' he said.

He cleared his throat, spat, and walked away. But I wasn't satisfied: this easy victory was too good to be true. I went out into the street and followed him for a bit, the gun in my pocket with my hand still on it. He'd almost reached the end of the Passage, where it opened into the rue Nationale, when he suddenly whirled round and crouched down to face me, eyes blazing. A pity to spoil his looks, but I dealt him a vigorous blow on the forehead with my revolver butt. He staggered, regained his balance, and charged. This time he wasn't alone: he was holding a flick-knife. I dodged the blade, grabbed his wrist with my left hand and gave his right hand a good thump with the butt of my gun, making him drop the knife. It clattered down on the cobblestones, and when I tried to kick it out of harm's way it slid under the door of Lenantais's shed, among the rags and bones.

'And now stop playing the fool,' I said. 'We've got an audience.'

A couple of Arab idlers had appeared, and were peering with interest into the alley from the rue Nationale. Salvador gave me an almighty shove that sent me flying against the door of the shed, then took to his heels. The Arabs looked disappointed. I shook myself and legged it back to Belita as fast as I could. Now Salvador knew I was sleeping with her we'd have to move. He'd be back soon with his pals. I was getting rather fed up with all this racism.

7 The stranger

A taxi took us to my place. Our recent agitations
called for a refreshing bath and a change of clothes.
From there I phoned my secretary, Hélène, to say I
was all right and might be away a bit longer. I also
asked if there was anything to report – any calls from
Florimond Faroux, for example? The other dear girl
said all was quiet on the office front. Then I rang
around the doctors I knew until I found one who
knew someone at the Salpêtrière. The contact was a
male nurse called Forest, recommended as resourceful,
reliable and discreet. Then I set off on the job. Belita
insisted on coming too, but though she knew some of
the people I planned to interview, and so might be
useful later on, I thought it best to pay the first of
my visits on my own.

Forest was a young fellow with the grave expression
of someone trying to get to grips with historical
materialism. I felt I could be frank with him, and told
him who I was and who had put me on to him.

'I'm looking for information about Benoit, the rag-
and-bone man who died here yesterday.'

'The anarchist?' he said, smiling.

I stopped him before we got into a discussion on the relative merits of anarchism and Marxism.

'Yes. I think he knew one of the doctors here. He may have asked for him when he was admitted. If so I'd like to know who it was. Is that possible?'

'Yes. Not right away, but some time during the day.'

'Here's my office number. Let my secretary know how you make out, either way.'

As I gave him my card I slipped him a banknote in case he was behind with his union dues (though this didn't seem very likely). But he nobly declined to take it.

I then rejoined Belita. She was leaning over the parapet on the quai d'Austerlitz, watching a freighter preparing to leave the port. She now took me to see Old Anselme, a colleague of Lenantais's in the old clothes trade. He lived and stored his goods in a wooden shack not far away on some waste land overlooking a stretch of old railway line. A dog barked and dragged at his chain as we approached the house through scattered heaps of junk. As Belita performed the introductions, Old Anselme eyed our clothes with a professional eye. I spun him a yarn about why I was interested in 'Benoit'. I don't know if he believed it.

'He was a good sort,' said the ancient. 'A hard worker, too. What was that I read in the paper about his having been a counterfeiter? I can't get over it . . . That must have been why they killed him.'

'Because he was once a counterfeiter?'

'No – because he was so industrious.'

'You mean it's a local custom for the drones to bump off the workers?'

'No – I mean I know whose fault it was if he was knifed.'

'Whose?'

'Joanovici's.'

My hopes faded.

'Yes, it's all because of Joanovici! Everybody thinks he's a millionaire as well as a rag-and-bone man, so they've got the idea we must all be rich. And as Benoit never stopped working they thought he must be even richer than the rest of us. So that was why he was attacked . . . He wasn't the first one, either. Did you know Marie? . . . No? And you, young lady? . . . No? Funny – I thought everyone knew Marie . . . Well, never mind. A month ago, because they thought she was rolling in money – pfffft!' He drew his hand swiftly across his throat. 'They cut her throat! Raped her too, what's more . . . Well, I don't want that to happen to me. That's why I've got a dog . . .'

If all Lenantais's friends were as dim as Anselme this case was going to last a month of Sundays.

They *were* all as dim as Anselme! – those we saw in the afternoon, as well as those we questioned towards evening. A fog that promised to be as bad as yesterday's started to creep over the city. Abel Benoit? Oh yes, of course – they knew him! But he kept himself to himself, so they left him alone too. Fancy his real name being Lenantais, and his having forged bank notes!

At least this proved they'd read Marc Covet's piece,

which had also, I'd discovered, been taken up in the other evening papers.

An anarchist too, was he? They weren't surprised. If ever he did express an opinion, at election time for instance, he trotted out some funny ideas. And what about the gipsy woman? What did he want to get mixed up with one of them for? Thieves, the lot of them!

This particular informant punctuated his words with swigs of rotgut. He was the only one who had anything but praise for Lenantais. What could you expect of someone who didn't drink? And who took up with a gipsy? And maybe didn't even sleep with her!

Either he did sleep with her and it was a scandal because of the difference in age and race. Or he didn't sleep with her and he was a fool.

I was glad to have done with the rag-and-bone men. They gave off a nasty smell, and it wasn't only physical.

By this time we were in the rue des Cinq-Diamants, and I phoned Hélène from a bistro on the corner. Had she heard anything from a chap called Forest? She hadn't.

We now made for the rue Watt, where Lenantais was supposed to have been attacked. I didn't expect to learn anything there, but what was another disappointment more or less?

It was a mugger's paradise. For about half its length it ran under a viaduct carrying several sets of railway lines and supported on rows of thin metal pillars. Extremely sinister, especially at dusk on a dark November day. A few faint street lights showed up the trickles of moisture running down the walls. As we walked along the pavement, fenced off by a railing from the road several feet below, a train thundered by overhead. But neither there nor in the rest of the street – the open stretch between the rue de la Croix-Jarry and the quai de la Gare, with houses on either side – did we find anything significant. We retraced our steps, accompanied this time by the noise of an interminable goods train.

We turned off left into the rue Cantagrel, where the workshops and offices of the Salvation Army occupied quite a lot of space. But I couldn't see Lenantais having much to do with that institution, except perhaps to enter into an ideological debate with its members. But the followers of William and Evangeline Booth weren't likely to have settled the argument with knives.

By now it was past dinner-time, and we made our way back to the Brasserie Rozès. Before sitting down I rang Hélène at home. Still no news of Forest. Or of anyone else.

I rang the Salpêtrière.

'Forest? Oh, he went off duty some time ago! He won't be in again till tomorrow morning . . . What? . . . There's no need to be rude!'

We ate in silence. It had been a depressing day.

'Let's go to the pictures, Belita,' I said as I picked up my change. 'There's a detective film on at the Palais-Italie. It may give me some ideas.'

It didn't.

'You know, Belita, I reckon the only person who

might – only might – be able to help us is that doctor at the Salpêtrière . . . the one he seems to have trusted enough to agree to be his patient . . . I was hoping Forest could find out the quack's name – always supposing old Lenantais actually got around to mentioning it – but maybe Forest isn't as resourceful as he's made out to be . . .'

She gave a stifled cry.

'*Madre de Dios!* The doctor!'

'What do you mean?'

'The doctor who came to see him one day! Oh, it was a long time ago. A couple of years or so. I've only just remembered. It may have been the same one . . . But I can't remember his name . . .'

'But if he wrote a prescription it would have been on headed paper . . . *Did* he write a prescription?'

'Yes – I took it to the chemist's myself.'

I grabbed her arm.

'Belita, we're going straight back to the Passage des Hautes-Formes! If Lenantais kept that prescription I'll find it, even if I have to look through every book in the place! The cops won't have paid any attention to it . . .'

I kept an eye open as we went along the Passage des Hautes-Formes, in case Dolores or Salvador was lurking about somewhere. But we got into Belita's courtyard without incident, and as before I lifted the latch of the little door leading into Lenantais's place. As before, it resisted. Perhaps the bundle of rags had rolled down again. Perhaps someone was in there, searching, and had knocked it down? The fact that we couldn't see any light coming from inside made no difference: the shed had no window, and even if there was anyone in there they might have turned the light off when they heard us at the door.

'I'll go in first,' I whispered. 'Where's the light switch?'

She told me. I got out my gun and went in. I almost tripped over the bundle of rags, but managed to find the light and switched it on. Then I looked around. The chaos was the same as before. And there was no one there.

No one living.

8 The wandering corpse

It wasn't a bundle of old rags that had prevented the door from opening properly. The sheepskin jacket, the waistcoat, trousers and shoes I looked down on were too good to be thrown in the dustbin. I put my gun away and dragged the body into the light. It was a man of about the same age as Lenantais, with small, deepset eyes that couldn't have been very affable when they were alive. The foxy face wore an expression of surprise mingled with incredulity: he hadn't been expecting to be stabbed in the back. That was what I saw had happened when I turned the body over: the blade had been driven right through the man's clothes and into his heart. Death must have been immediate. Belita gave a little moan. She'd started to follow me, but having caught sight of the body was clinging, ashen-faced, to a tottering pile of junk. After a moment she turned aside and was violently sick.

'It's nothing,' I said. 'You've only known me for twenty-four hours. A few months from now you'll be used to it, and realize corpses are meat and drink to me . . . And now to business. Be a brave girl – take a look at this fellow and tell me if you know him.'

I turned the corpse over on its back again.

She overcame her reluctance and leaned forward.

'I've never set eyes on him before,' she breathed, straightening up and averting her gaze.

'Right. Maybe he's got some papers on him.'

I explored his pockets. Nothing. No papers, no cigarettes, no money. I went and shut the little door we'd carelessly left open, then walked over to the shed's main entrance. That door too was slightly ajar. I examined the floor. Salvador's knife ought to have been there. There or underneath Lenantais's old Ford. But it was nowhere to be seen.

'Salvador's been here again, Belita,' I said. 'Either to get his dagger back, or to kill me, or both. He must have found the other chap ferreting about and taken him for me because of the sheepskin jacket. He could easily have been mistaken, looking at the target from behind and at a distance . . . And I suppose he's pretty good at throwing knives?'

'Yes!'

She shuddered.

'Well, he hit the bull's-eye all right, and when he discovered he'd got the wrong guy he consoled himself by picking his pockets.'

I looked at the body. Who was this man, and what had he been doing here? I gave the whole place a quick once-over, trying to make out where the victim had been standing when he was dispatched. As I searched I spotted an evening paper lying on the floor. It must have been brought there either by the dead man or by Salvador. The former, evidently, because it was that day's *Crépu*, folded open at Marc Covet's article on Albert Lenantais. So in a way *I* was responsible for this second old buffer's death.

'The cops mustn't find him here,' I said. 'There's no need for them to know he was interested in our friend. But I do want to identify him, and the police will do that faster and better than I can. So we'll wait for a bit and then I'll stow him away somewhere where he won't decay too fast. It's a risk worth taking. Meanwhile let's have a look for that prescription . . .'

I covered the corpse with a sheet, then Belita and I went upstairs and searched. No luck. I looked at my watch, then checked that the Passage was empty and the fog grown nice and thick.

'Does the van still go, Belita? I can't carry him on my back.'

The old Ford hadn't yet given up the ghost, the girl said, and with her help I managed to get the body into the back. It wasn't an easy task. Very brave of her to lend a hand. And when I took my place behind the wheel she slipped into the passenger seat. She intended to come with me. A strongminded girl, Belita, and once she'd made up her mind about something, that was that.

We bumped over the cobbles and out into the rue Nationale, then turned right into the rue de Tolbiac and left towards the river. At the intersection with the rue de Patay another late driver nearly crashed into us. Silly idiot! Admittedly the Ford's headlights weren't exactly dazzling, but what did the fathead think he was doing, driving around at this time of night? As was got nearer the river the fog grew denser and more penetrating. My fingers, clutching tightly at the wheel, were numb with cold as well as strain. But the sweat was pouring off me just the same. Belita's trembling thigh sometimes brushed against mine, and I could tell from that, and from the scent of her, that she was sweating too. What an excursion! I only hoped no one would look in the back of the van . . . When were we going to reach the river? Did it still exist? . . . But it was too late now to draw back.

Ahead through the sooty haze I could hear the muffled rumble of a train. The pont de Tolbiac! The iron bridge spanning the main-line rails of the Gare d'Austerlitz! Nearly there at last! Then . . .

Another blasted road-hog! Drunk, no doubt. Or English. Or both. He was driving on the left, without lights, and by the time it dawned on him that a bit of illumination wouldn't do any harm he was on top of us! It was like a flash of lightning! Before I was totally dazzled I saw the moisture of the fog turn iridescent in the glare of the other car's powerful head-lamps. I wrenched desperately at the wheel, the van mounted the pavement, and there was a deafening clatter of smashing coach-work as we came to rest against a wall. The other driver swerved off to the right and drove away. Just as well. I sat there for a moment, stunned. Belita had been thrown on to the floor. I helped her up. We didn't speak. I took out my handkerchief and mopped my brow. In front of us the yellow-painted mass of the cold storage depot loomed faintly through the fog. Below, a train moved blindly along, jolting over the points, echoing through the silence. I pulled myself together. We couldn't stay here indefinitely. I tried to start up the engine. Not a flicker. God, were we going to have to go away and leave the corpse behind? There was a starting handle under the seat. I seized it, leapt out, and at the first attempt succeeded only in giving myself a nasty bang on the wrist. I tried again. The engine gave a short snigger, then stalled. My head filled with imaginary sounds: engines turning over, footsteps in the street, cars approaching, sirens shrieking. My last attempt succeeded. I ought to have started with that one. I jumped back into the van and stepped on the gas, in more of a hurry than ever to deposit our cargo in some quiet spot where it would easily be found.

When we emerged on to the quai de la Gare it was deserted except for a few tramps sleeping over hot-air shafts. An icy shroud of vapour lay over the Seine, and over the Bercy wine depot on the opposite bank. I drove the Ford, now rattling worse than before, down the first slope we came to that led down to the river bank. There was a lot of old iron lying about: a scrap yard. Our friend seemed interested in junk: he should feel at home here. I stopped, hopped out, ran round to the back of the van and felt around for the body. The crash and the jolting around had probably moved it a bit. I groped with both arms outspread. I hadn't heard Belita join me, and when she put her hand on my shoulder I nearly jumped out of my skin. It took me about a century to find my matches. I struck one . . . The body had vanished.

Belita's legs gave way. I just caught her before she fell.

'Never mind,' I told her. 'We'll soon find another one.'

I helped her back into the van and started the engine.

'What are we going to do?' she asked.

'Take this old jalopy back where it came from, for a start . . .'

I began to retrace our route. In the middle of the pont de Tolbiac I thought I could see the beam of a powerful torch piercing the fog some distance ahead. I accelerated, to make sure, drove past, and then accelerated some more. Yes, two figures in capes had been bending over a shape lying huddled on the pavement.

'A police patrol,' I said. 'And our dear departed. The flap at the back of this rattle-trap must have come loose when I swerved to avoid that road-hog. And our corpse must have fallen out.'

When we were safely back in the Passage des Haute-Formes I parked the van and wiped down all the parts where we might have left finger-prints. Then, after Belita had made herself less conspicuous by taking off her ear-rings and tying a scarf over her hair, we ventured forth into the empty streets. We found a taxi in the Place d'Italie and drove to my place.

I fell on the whisky bottle. Belita, true to Lenantais's principles, refused a drink. I downed enough for two, and we hit the hay.

9 *The corpse reveals its secret*

We didn't sleep the sleep of the just. I lay awake thinking of that wretched stiff, and Belita's slumbers seemed to be haunted by Salvador. I suppose that's what they mean by division of labour.

'I'm sorry, I'm sorry!' she sobbed at one point. 'Don't kill him, Salvador – don't kill him!'

And she turned in her sleep and clung to me. I held her tight and murmured something soothing. She gradually calmed down, but still moaned every so often. All this trouble was too much for a kid of her age, even if she was a gipsy. It was too much for me too.

But I'd get the better of it, and something told me our recent passenger would unwittingly help me do so. The hands of the bedside clock showed just after five. I decided I'd wait for an hour and then get up and have a bath and a drink: that would either worsen my hang-over or cure it. Anyhow it was worth a try. But Belita's nightmare seemed to have exorcized her fears: she was breathing softly and regularly now. I didn't want to disturb her by slipping out of bed . . . I drowsed off too, and we didn't wake up till ten.

A ray of wan November sunshine shone in between the curtains. What did today have in store? Don't even ask, Nestor – just go and make some coffee. I did as I'd told me and brought Belita a cup. She sat up in a charmingly tousled set of my pyjamas, and stared for a while into space.

'I believe I may manage to be of use to you in the end, darling,' she said at last with a faint smile, after she'd drunk her coffee. 'I long to help you find the swine who killed poor Benoit, but I'm so afraid of not knowing how, of not being clever enough . . .'

'Nonsense, my love!'

She pressed my hand.

' "My love!" ' she mused sadly. Then went on:

'Maybe there are things I know, or did know, but I shan't remember them in time to help you . . . Like that business about the doctor . . . It wasn't any use to you, was it? . . . I ought to have remembered it sooner.'

'Not any use? It helped us find a corpse!'

She shuddered.

'You think that was bad?' I said. 'On the contrary – it was probably the best thing that could have happened . . . Believe me! I've had plenty of experience!'

'I still ought to have thought of it before.'

'No use crying over spilt milk. If you'd remembered sooner we'd have gone to the Passage des Hautes-Formes sooner, and I might have been the one who ran into Salvador. And then I wouldn't have been here to listen to you reproaching yourself.'

'Salvador,' she murmured. Her gold-flecked brown eyes were suddenly full of fear.

'Talking of him,' I said, 'you mustn't have any more nightmares like the ones you had last night. And you mustn't keep saying you're sorry. What have you done that you need apologize for?'

'Lots of things,' she whispered, hanging her head.

I stroked the back of her neck beneath her thick black hair.

'He won't kill me, darling. No need to worry about me on that account. I don't suppose knifing the wrong person made him give up on me, but I reckon he means to lie low. He had enough nerve to rob his victim, but not enough to try to hide the body, and he must have realized it'd be found eventually . . . I reckon he and Dolores and their pals have made tracks. Where do they usually hang out?'

'Near Ivry.'

'I'll go and have a look round.'

'No!' she cried. 'You mustn't! Please! You mustn't!'

'All right, I won't.'

I gave her a kiss.

'I'm sure they'll have moved on, anyway. A murder's a murder, even for a gipsy . . . But that's enough about him. What were you saying . . . ?'

'I was talking about my awful memory. Look how long it took me to remember it was in the rue Watt that Benoit was attacked . . .'

'Where he *said* he was attacked. He was secretive enough when I knew him, but he seems to have got worse as he grew older.'

'But supposing he was telling the truth about the rue Watt . . . ?'

'You want us to go back there? But we had a good look yesterday . . .'

'No, I don't want to go back there exactly. But we did pass by the Salvation Army place. And I've just remembered . . . Benoit did have some dealings with the Salvation Army lately. They have some workshops where they teach down-and-outs to mend furniture, and he sold them some bits and pieces . . .'

I laughed.

'And they quarrelled over the price, or over religion, and they knifed him! . . . I've already considered that theory. But it doesn't square with what he said in his letter.'

'All right, make fun of me,' she said sadly. 'You *do* think I'm stupid!'

'Of course I don't, darling. But clues don't just drop out of the sky, you know – you have to feel your way towards them. You're just feeling your way still, that's all.'

Shortly after that I went out and got the papers. No mention of the police having found a corpse on the pont de Tolbiac.

'Someone phoned,' said Belita when I got back. 'She said she was your secretary.'

I called Hélène.

'Well, hallo!' she said. 'I tried to ring you five minutes ago but I must have got a wrong number. It was a woman who answered. A young woman, to judge by her voice. It wasn't a very pretty voice, but it was *very* young.'

'It's just a kid who didn't have anywhere to sleep.'

'So you took her in. How kind and charitable. A kid, eh? Quite right not to leave her on the street, with so many dirty old men about. So now I know why you haven't shown up in the office lately . . .'

'You can pass the explanation on to Faroux if he's worried about me. Has he been in touch?'

'No.'

'Good.'

'But I did have a call just now from someone called Forest.'

'At last! Well, what did he say?'

'He didn't seem very talkative. He just passed on a name. Dr Emile Coudérat. But I expect that's enough for you to go on?'

'I hope so.'

I wrote it down.

'Thanks very much, Hélène. See you!'

'So long, Abbé Pierre!'

I turned to Belita.

'Does the name Coudérat mean anything to you? Is it anything like the name on the prescription?'

She looked doubtful.

'I don't know. I can't remember.'

'Never mind. Anyhow, it's the name of the doctor our friend Lenantais asked for the night he was admitted to hospital.'

I phoned the Salpêtrière and asked for him.

'Hold on, please.'

Then a deep voice said:

'Hallo? Dr Coudérat doesn't practise here any more.'

I looked the name up in the telephone directory and found it at an address in the boulevard Arago. A very suitable address for a quack. I dialled the number.

93

'Dr Coudérat, please.'

'He's not here at the moment. Did you want to make an appointment?'

'Er . . . yes, in a way.'

'Would three this afternoon be convenient?'

'Yes, please. The name's Burma. Nestor Burma. But could I call back and have a word with the doctor beforehand?'

'You could try at lunch-time.'

'Do you happen to know if he ever practised at the Salpêtrière?'

'I'm afraid I couldn't say.'

'Never mind. Thank you.'

At midday I bought the first editions of all the evening papers and read them from end to end. Not a line about my mysterious corpse. After all I'd done to make him known . . .

At around one I called the doctor's number again. He answered the phone himself. I explained that I had an appointment but that to avoid wasting his time I was ringing to ask if he'd ever worked at the Salpêtrière . . .

'Yes . . . But I don't quite see . . . Oh well, perhaps . . . What is it that's wrong with you exactly?'

'Nothing. I'm as fit as a fiddle. But I'm a private detective and I want to speak to you professionally. I'm down to come to your place at three, but I was wondering if you could see me briefly before you start your consultations . . .'

He agreed to see me for a few minutes at ten to two.

'No point in your coming with me,' I told Belita.

'You stay here in the warm. Help yourself to books and fags and gramophone records.'

I bought the latest edition of the *Crépu* as I went along. Would there be a mention of my dead body at last?

Hell and damnation! The big black headline read:

PONT DE TOLBIAC CLAIMS POLICE INSPECTOR AGAIN.

I scanned the article.

'At about 3.30 a.m. today, near the entrance to the pont de Tolbiac in the 13th arrondissement, a police patrol discovered the body of a man who had been stabbed to death and robbed. He was soon identified as Monsieur Norbert Ballin, aged fifty-five, a retired inspector of police. This was the second time he had fallen victim to the pont de Tolbiac. In 1936 he was in charge of a case concerning the mysterious disappearance of a large sum of money, together with that of the messenger transporting it, a Monsieur Daniel. The money belonged to the Cold Storage Company, which owns premises on the quai de la Gare nearby, and it has never been established whether the messenger himself ran away with the cash or whether he was the victim of a gang of thieves. He was last seen one evening in December 1936 on the pont de Tolbiac.

'Despite unremitting efforts, Inspector Ballin was never able to solve the mystery. In his attempts to do so he made use of many of his usual informers from among the criminal classes, some of whom he "blew", possibly in the hope of stirring things up and uncovering a pointer towards a solution. But that hope was vain. However, for the Inspector the case was never closed, and from that time on he interrogated every criminal who came his way in the hope of trapping them into giving him some clue. But they never did. The constant strain and disappointment undermined Inspector Ballin's physical and mental health. He was deported by the Germans during the war, and took early retirement when he returned to France from Buchenwald. But still, according to friends and colleagues, he went on haunting the scene of the crime in the hope of solving the mystery of the pont de Tolbiac. It was there he fell victim to last night's fatal attack by prowlers as yet unidentified. Local residents have frequently called for official measures to be taken against this scourge.'

Outside Dr Coudérat's stylish little mansion in the boulevard Arago, midway between the Santé prison and the hôpital Broca, I nearly bumped into a wealthy old dowager who'd just got out of a limousine. We were both ushered into the waiting room by a maid in a white apron, but I was the first to be summoned to the doctor's spacious panelled consulting room on the first floor. A ray of sunshine was trying to brighten up the garden below, but it hadn't a hope. Coudérat was a slim, elegant, middle-aged man beginning to go thin on top and wearing glasses with rims invisible to the naked eye. They made you feel you were the one who was shortsighted.

'I've never met a private detective before,' he said, after our hands had exchanged microbes. (Amazing the number of witnesses who start off with this bromide, accompanied by smiles of interest and delight. The influence of the cinema, I suppose. They sometimes change their tune later on.) 'Do sit down . . . How can I be of use to you?'

'It's about a man called Albert Lenantais,' I said. 'Or Abel Benoit – I don't know which name you knew him by. Anyhow, he knew you. He was stabbed twice a few days ago in the street, and the wounds proved fatal. He'd asked to be taken to the Salpêtrière because he hoped that you were still there.'

Dr Coudérat frowned.

'What did you say the name was?'

'Albert Lenantais or Abel Benoit. He was a very good sort, but he had two identities. His past might have been considered rather dubious, too, depending on your point of view. It was all in the papers.'

'I don't usually read that sort of thing.'

'He was a rag-and-bone man and lived in the Passage des Hautes-Formes. You visited him there professionally a couple of years ago. As your patients seem to come from rather a different social class, I deduced that you must have known him personally.'

'Is that what you came to ask me?'

'Yes.'

He took off his specs and polished them.

'Hmmm,' he said, putting them on again. 'I see who you mean. A nice chap. Rather eccentric.'

'Yes. He'd had himself tattooed . . .'

'Yes.'

A pause.

'I didn't know him personally. A friend and patient of mine took an interest in him, and asked me to go and see him.'

'And what was your friend's name?'

He coughed.

'This is rather awkward. I'm not an information bureau, and I don't know what it is you want with my friend.'

'I want to warn him.'

'Warn him? Against what?'

'Now it's my turn to be reticent – I have to be as discreet as I can. But I can tell you that your friend, if he was Lenantais's friend too, is in danger – mortal danger. Of course, as a doctor, you're probably not too worried at one death more or less . . .'

He neither laughed nor lost his temper.

'Listen, Monsieur Burma, this is more a matter of etiquette than of confidentiality. I'd like to have a word with my friend before we go any further.'

I stood up and nodded towards the phone.

'By all means. I'll leave you for a moment.'

And with that demonstration of good breeding I went and smoked a pipe in a corridor, passing the time by admiring a copy of *The Anatomy Lesson*. After a while the door of the consulting room opened.

'Please come in.'

I did so. Coudérat looked relieved.

'Monsieur Charles Baurénot has no objection to seeing you. On the contrary – he's waiting for you now. Would you care to write down the address?'

I walked down the boulevard Arago to the carrefour des Gobelins, where I bought an armful of evening papers. The police don't usually share their secret thoughts with the press, but occasionally you can detect something in the air if you know how to read between the lines. I'd have dearly liked to know if the cops had any original ideas about the death of ex-Inspector Ballin. But there was nothing to this effect in *France-Soir*, *Paris-Presse*, or *L'Information*. And the *Crépu* only had what I'd seen before. They all rambled on, with an undertone of facetiousness, about the former cop's woes, but attributed his death to ordinary prowlers. Of course it wasn't likely to occur to the police that a gipsy jealous for the honour of his race might have knifed him in mistake for someone else. Still less that poor old Ballin might have found out something about his Tolbiac mystery 'twenty years after', and been killed for his pains. But you never know.

Anyway, it was very odd that Ballin should have come poking around Lenantais's premises, apparently after reading the article that I'd got Marc Covet to write. Granted the ex-inspector was more than slightly touched, but even so . . .

As I ruminated on all this I turned into the rue Berbier-du-Mets and walked along as far as the Gobelins tapestry factory. I could see the tops of the looms through the windows. The Baurénot Company was opposite. Baurénot was a timber merchant, and the sound of an electric saw disturbed the provincial peace of the little winding street. I tried a wicket gate in the main entrance, but it wouldn't open until I found a button and pressed it. A porter then emerged from a small lodge, gazing first at his watch and then at the newspapers under my arm. Perhaps he thought I'd come to try to sell them.

'Monsieur Baurénot is expecting me,' I said, to clarify the situation.

'Just in time,' said the porter, glancing again at his wrist. 'If you'd been a minute later I'm not sure I'd have let you in.'

The electric saw suddenly stopped. A strange silence fell.

'Why not?' I asked. 'Have you made some sort of a vow?'

He tilted his head to one side.

'Do you hear that saw?'

'I've just stopped hearing it!'

'That's what I mean. It's zero hour . . . We're on strike . . .'

He scratched his head vigorously.

'And I don't know how far I'm meant to be involved . . . No one's told me if I'm supposed to let people in and out or not.'

'Ask the strike committee.'

'Yes, I think I will . . . Meanwhile, as you're here and you say Monsieur Baurénot's expecting you . . . It's over there.'

I went up a few steps to an office with 'Director' on the door, where a secretary asked me to go upstairs. Upstairs another secretary, typing furiously to show she wasn't taking part in the strike, desisted long enough to take my card into the adjoining room and then ask me to go in. It was a comfortable room with a wood stove burning. A man of about fifty – fat, broad-shouldered, well dressed – stood by the window looking out through the net curtains into the factory yard. He looked vexed, to put it mildly. The workers were gathered together below; you could hear the hum of their voices. Monsieur Baurénot tore himself away from the depressing spectacle, turned on his elegant heel and looked me up and down. Like the porter, he seemed interested in my armful of papers. Then he suddenly flung out his arms and came towards me.

'Nestor Burma!' he cried, as joyfully as the circumstances allowed. 'How are you, old boy? Long time no see!'

10 Friends

He was levering my arm up and down as if I was a petrol pump. I must have shown my surprise.

'Don't you recognize your friends any more?' he said jovially, showing a fair number of gold teeth. 'Oh, I suppose it was the name that foxed you! – I didn't like to say too much to Dr Coudérat, but of course I didn't call myself Baurénot when you and I first met.'

'My God!' I exclaimed. 'Bernis! Camille Bernis!'

He put a finger to his lips.

'Ssh! Not so loud! Camille Bernis is dead and buried – don't let's disturb him . . . As a matter of fact he never existed!'

'Steady on! I can't keep up with you. You seem to change your name as often as other people change their shirt!'

He laughed.

'Bernis never was my real name. My real name is the one I use now, perfectly respectably. But in the old days, among the anars, they didn't ask you for your identity card, and for family and other reasons I chose to call myself Bernis. Then, later on, when

I . . . er . . . settled down, all I had to do was turn into Charles Baurénot again.'

'Very clever,' I said.

'Yes,' he sighed. He went over and looked down into the yard again, where the workers were holding some kind of a meeting.

'You need to be clever to get the better of that lot,' he said. He turned back to me. 'I've become a capitalist, you see. I inherited this business, and I've built it up and made it prosper. And you can't make an omelette—'

'—without breaking eggs! . . . I know!' I grinned.

A grimmish silence followed.

'One's point of view changes . . .' he said. 'But I take it you don't care for that kind of talk?'

I waved my hand in a gesture that might have meant anything.

He smiled.

'And you . . . you've become a cop!'

'A private one. There's a difference.'

'If you say so. Ah well, what's done is done. People don't change any more at our age.'

We both sat down. He lit a Gitane and toyed with a paper-knife. A phone rang at some length in the next room.

'I've often seen your name in the papers,' he said.

There was a knock at the door.

'Come in!'

The strike-breaking secretary put her pretty little nose round the door.

'It's about the new machines being shipped to us,' she said. 'The harbour people at Austerlitz . . .'

'I'm busy. You see to it, please . . .'

'And then there's the spokesman of the . . .'

'I'll see him later.'

'Yes, monsieur.'

She disappeared. Baurénot growled to himself. Then:

'I sometimes used to wonder, when I read about you in the papers, if you were the same chap as the one I knew long ago.'

'You didn't talk about it to Lenantais? *He* wasn't in any doubt!'

'Not really . . . Anyhow, I never tried to get in touch with you. That's one way I'm still just the same: I don't like bothering other people, and I don't like them bothering me.'

That sounded a bit threatening, but perhaps it wasn't meant for present company. As he spoke he seemed to have one ear on what was happening outside.

'The trouble is,' I answered, 'you can't always stop people bothering you.'

He gave me a look.

'Meaning?'

'Meaning that some day one of those bothersome people might pay you a visit . . . And I'm not referring to myself!'

He shook his head.

'I don't understand.'

'Neither do I. But I'm trying.'

I got out my pipe and lit it.

'Lenantais wasn't set upon by North Africans, as the papers said and as everyone else believes, including the police. In our old friend's own words, it was "some bastard up to no good" who stabbed him. And that bastard . . .'

And I put him in the picture about Lenantais's message.

'At first,' I added, 'he intended to tell you what had happened through Dr Coudérat. But the doctor wasn't at the Salpêtrière any more. So then Lenantais thought of me – partly because he believed I could be trusted, and partly perhaps because he reckoned I might be better than most at thwarting the bastard's intentions. He deliberately left his young gipsy protégée out of it – all she had to do was post me his letter. I answered his appeal without knowing who he was. I didn't know any Abel Benoit. Why did he change his name?'

'He thought his revolutionary past might get him into trouble during the Occupation. He wasn't a rag-and-bone man in those days – I don't know what he was doing. Anyhow, for some reason or other he started to call himself Abel Benoit, and he went on using the name afterwards . . . And so by the time you got to the hospital he was dead?'

'Yes.'

We said nothing more for a while. Baurénot was thinking. Occasionally there was a gleam in his eye that reminded me of our discussions long ago, in the Rebels' Club and the dormitory at the Vegan Centre . . . The sound of the union meeting still wafted up from below.

'Well, then,' he resumed in his managing director's voice, as if rehearsing a confrontation with the strike committee. 'Well, then. Some son of a bitch murders Lenantais. This son of a bitch has also got it in for some of Lenantais's friends, so he asks you to help them. Is that it? . . . Right. And you thought straight away I must be the one in danger?'

'You . . . someone else . . . several people . . . I don't know. I got to you through the link with Dr Coudérat. But Lenantais may have meant other friends . . .'

'He did mean other friends. I don't say I haven't got any enemies – ' he glanced towards the window, ' – but I can't think of anyone who'd really want to do me any harm.'

'Good for you. So now we must try to find the friends Lenantais *did* mean. They must be good guys . . . Lenantais was one himself.'

'Yes,' said Baurénot. Then added with a condescending smile: 'But rather naïve . . . We still arranged to meet occasionally. And sometimes we ran into one another by chance. He was very amusing. He still hung on to so many of the old ideas. I'd have liked to help him, but he'd never take anything. His quiet little life was enough for him – he liked to be free and independent. I sent Coudérat to see him one day when I knew he was ill, and he insisted on paying. Not like some of our old friends, who used to decamp in the morning with the alarm clock or the sheets of the people who'd given them a bed.'

'No, he certainly wasn't like them. Do you know if he saw any other old friends besides you?'

'I'm sure he didn't.'

'And what about you? Did you keep in touch with any of them?'

'No . . . I severed all connections a long time ago. Why do you ask?'

'Because you might know the people who are threatened. Lenantais might have chosen you just as an intermediary.'

'No,' said Baurénot. 'I'm not in danger, and I don't know anybody who might be. And what's more . . .' he grimaced, '. . . I'm not sure old Lenantais wasn't a bit cracked. I ask you, is it normal to live as he did? No, he was definitely odd, and so was his message, and so is all the rest of it . . .'

'No,' said I. 'He wasn't cracked. I'm sure of it.'

He shrugged.

'Have it your own way. What else do you want to know?'

'I'd like you to tell me why you and Lenantais went on seeing each other. I wouldn't have thought you still had much in common.'

He seemed to shrink a little, and bowed his head. When he looked up at me again there was pain in his eyes.

'I don't know . . .' His hand tightened round the handle of the paper-knife. 'If Lenantais wasn't mad, perhaps I am. I sometimes found myself envying him. Oh, I know rich people are always saying that sort of thing. But with me it's different. There was something pure about Lenantais – it did you good to see it. That's why I went on seeing him, even if it wasn't very often. And that's why, one day when I met him and he said he felt ill and was going home to bed, I asked Coudérat to go and see him. I didn't care what the quack thought about the boss of Baurénot and Co. being friendly with a rag-and-bone man. He thought I was just being kind. But it wasn't charity.'

'It was attachment to the past,' I told him. 'It was because of what we believed when we were young. Whatever you become afterwards you never quite forget that.'

'Yes,' he sighed. 'The past . . . Youth . . .' Then he took hold of himself and became more aggressive. 'Oh well, the past is the past. We're not going to start theorizing and splitting hairs again at our time of life. To hell with the past, I say!'

At that point the door burst open and a man stormed in.

'You see?' said the newcomer with an oath.

Then he noticed me, and stopped. He was a craggy-faced type, smartly turned out and wearing gold-rimmed glasses. But his brown eyes had a feverish, hunted expression, and he looked as if he might pass out at any moment.

'Terrific!' said Baurénot sardonically. 'Now there are enough of us to form a committee and tell those idiots out there how to usher in the revolution . . . Don't you recognize Deslandes, Burma?'

'I only knew him as Jean,' I said, getting up. 'But the way the past has kept cropping up lately, I think I'd recognize anyone connected with the old Vegan Centre.'

'Burma!' cried the ex-deserter, who seemed to have come to terms with society since the old days, and to have left our old world far behind. He'd made progress. Everybody had . . . 'Well, *I* wouldn't have recognized *you*! Of course, you were only a lad at the time.'

We shook hands. I noticed his was clammy.

'So we're older than Burma is,' joked Baurénot. 'And he ought to treat us with respect.'

Jean Deslandes turned to him.

'The porter almost refused to let me in . . . So the bastards are on strike, are they?'

'Yes . . . It's the time of year . . . But what's the matter? Aren't you feeling well?'

'I must have eaten something that didn't agree with me,' said Deslandes, clutching at his stomach. 'Oysters, I think.'

He found a chair and sat down. The workers were still arguing away outside. There was a knock at the door, Baurénot yelled 'Come in!', and the secretary did so.

'They're getting impatient, monsieur,' she said.

'All right, I'll go down and see them,' said Baurénot wearily. 'I'll leave you two lads together. You must have a lot to tell each other.'

He went out. But we didn't have much to say. Deslandes finally broke the silence.

'What a laugh,' he said. 'Who'd have thought there'd ever be people on strike against one of us? Don't you think it's funny?'

'Not very,' I said.

I felt tired and sad. A bit embarrassed too.

'That's that, my friends!' said Baurénot triumphantly, coming back into the room. 'Listen! The sound of honest toil once more!'

As he spoke the electric saw had started up again.

'Has it all been sorted out, then?' Deslandes asked.

'Everything can be sorted out somehow!' said Baurénot. 'We must never despair! I've agreed to the men's demands – they were quite legitimate, as it happens, and I'm not such a bad chap really.'

'And it's just as well to be on the side of the angels, eh?' said Deslandes bitterly.

'Since you mention angels, I believe there's one who

looks after drunks. And what with the end of the strike and our all getting together again, I think it's time for a little celebration, don't you?'

He vanished briefly and came back with three glasses and a bottle of champagne.

'To the health of the Vegan Centre,' he said.

We drank the toast, and Baurénot turned to Deslandes.

'Friend Burma came to see me about Lenantais,' he said.

I went over the story again for the benefit of the newcomer. He hadn't got anything useful to add, and the conversation became general. But I didn't feel I was wasting my time. I had a question to ask, but I was waiting for the right moment. I discovered that my two companions were both married, that Baurénot had a grown-up daughter, and that he and Deslandes were now regarded by one and all as respectable citizens. And so they were, now. Nobody suspected they'd ever professed subversive opinions. Like Baurénot, Deslandes was in business, and he too had done well. In short, poor old Lenantais was the only one who'd stuck to the old ideas.

'We've all changed,' I said. 'But that's life. I wonder what's become of the chap we used to call the Poet – I never did know his real name.'

'Perhaps he's been made a member of the Academy,' suggested Baurénot.

'Why not? . . . Anyhow, I trust potty old Barbapoux, the pipe-breaker, the one who wanted everyone to go down on all fours and eat grass, is kicking up daisies now. He was pretty ancient even then. And I must say I feel the same about Lacorre. He was always getting at me.'

'Lacorre!' cried Deslandes, as if he'd just sat on a drawing-pin.

'What's the matter?' I asked.

'Jean's rather prejudiced.' Baurénot seemed to be trying, rather laboriously, to make a joke of it. 'He accepts that people change – he even admits they may turn their coats. But he reckons Lacorre went a bit too far.'

'How do you mean?'

'Lacorre won't be getting at you any more. He's not dead yet, at least as far as I know, but he might just as well be – a provincial court handed him out a good stiff sentence.'

'What?' I laughed. 'Do you mean to say he wasn't just boasting and he really did attack a bank messenger?'

'No – it's funnier, or rather more sinister, than that. We only found out about it from the papers – he wasn't the kind of person we cared to see very often. Anyhow, at the end of 1936 he killed the woman he lived with because she was being unfaithful to him . . .'

'All in the name of free love, no doubt? For him, I mean – not her.'

'Exactly.'

'Well, it doesn't surprise me.'

'The jury had a nice sense of humour. "You claim to believe in free love," they said, "but as soon as your girlfriend's unfaithful you kill her? Well, we don't call that an ordinary crime of passion, and you can go to jail for ten years! No arguments!" They added another couple of years for his subversive ideas, not to mention a few other peccadilloes: he'd taken a pot-shot at the police when they came to arrest him.'

'What a dope!' said Deslandes, mopping his brow.

It was time to produce my bombshell.

'Talking of 1936 and bank messengers,' I said. 'I'd like you to tell me something about the pont de Tolbiac affair. It was you who killed the man with the money, wasn't it?'

11 Burial-ground

Deslandes huddled down in his chair. Baurénot said nothing, but when he poured himself what remained of the champagne the bottle clinked against the glass. In the workshop on the other side of the yard the electric saw went on producing profits. I didn't repeat my question; I just waited. Baurénot gave an affected laugh, enough to set your teeth on edge worse than the screech of the saw.

'That's a nice thing to say, Burma!' he protested. 'We've never bumped anyone off, on the pont de Tolbiac or anywhere else. What *is* the pont de Tolbiac affair, anyway?'

'You know more about it than I do,' I said with a sigh. 'But I'll give you a general idea if you like.'

'Don't bother. I tell you again – we haven't bumped anyone off.'

'Frankly, I don't think you did kill Daniel, the Cold Storage messenger. Lenantais was going to take part in the robbery, and I know his principles: strictly no bloodshed. And it was with your help he finally set up the job he'd had in mind for so long. But maybe the messenger was in cahoots with you . . . Hey, that gives me an idea!'

Then – while keeping my latest inspiration to myself – I told them what I'd read in the papers about that day in the winter of 1936.

'Very interesting,' Baurénot commented. 'And you suspect us of being responsible?'

'Why not?'

'Why not, indeed? Especially,' he said with heavy sarcasm, 'as there's such strong evidence against us: don't we live and carry on our business in the neighbourhood where the crime took place? . . . Do you always conduct your cases so brilliantly? . . . Why pick on perfectly respectable business men? Wouldn't gangsters be more likely?'

'For various reasons the pont de Tolbiac case doesn't sound like the work of gangsters . . . And by the way, ex-Inspector Norbert Ballin, who sweated blood over the affair and could never solve it, was stabbed to death the other night.'

'And we're responsible for that as well, are we?'

'Why not?'

They both shook their heads vehemently.

'Oh no,' said Baurénot. 'You're wrong there!'

I was well aware of that. But what I'd wanted to do was test his protestations. And while his denial of responsibility for the Ballin murder sounded – with good reason – quite genuine, his disavowals of the earlier crimes were obviously false.

'All right,' I said. 'But to come back to Ballin, there was an interesting reference to him in the papers after his death . . .'

Deslandes interrupted.

'The papers!' he sneered.

'Don't try to pretend they're beneath your notice!

Your waistcoat pocket is bulging with cuttings! And isn't that because Ballin's death has made them dig up the old pont de Tolbiac affair? And isn't it because the revival of the case scares you stiff that you've come running here to consult with Baurénot? Baurénot, who doesn't mix with people much these days, but who sees Deslandes all right and used to see Lanantais as well! I notice there are plenty of newspapers on Baurénot's desk, too, and he could hardly take his eyes off the bundle I had under my arm when I came in . . . Of course, he may merely have inserted a small ad., but just the same it's funny the three of us be so interested in the press all of a sudden . . .'

'Hold on,' said Baurénot. 'I know someone who buys fifteen newspapers every day. That's neither here nor there . . . But what was the reference about Ballin that struck you?'

I looked it up in the *Crépuscule*.

'It says that though he "made use of his usual informers from among the criminal classes" he didn't get any help. Now that strikes me as significant. When a gangster steps too far out of line he's usually shopped pretty soon by some other members of the criminal classes. Only loners who don't belong to the underworld can hope to get away with their misdeeds. And the people with the best chance of all are the anarchists. They're capable of lying low for as long as is necessary; they don't go boozing and spilling the beans; and because they see as few other people as possible, the chances of betrayal are limited. Besides, the anars are different . . . and the lack of clues, the inadequacy of the informers, and one other little detail that I prefer to keep to myself – all these things

suggest to me that the pont de Tolbiac affair was due
to one or more intellectual bandits.'

'Intellectual bandits?' exclaimed Baurénot.

'Yes! And I don't mean it negatively. You used the
expression often enough yourself in the days when you
professed subversive opinions.'

' "Professed"? We merely discussed them. Everybody did.'

'Well, anyway, you know what I mean. May I go
on with the story now? Stop me if I get anything
wrong.'

'What's the point? Everything you say will be
wrong!'

'Very well – just listen. You two and Lenantais got
round the messenger and then divided up the swag
between the four of you. Sorry I can't go into detail
– I wasn't actually there—'

'Nor were we!'

'Daniel, the messenger, fled abroad. At any rate, he
disappeared from view. And you three went on with
your lives in accordance with your various tastes. And
then all of a sudden Daniel pops up again! That's the
idea that struck me a little while ago, and I'll now
give you the benefit of it. He didn't know your names
– you'd changed them – but for some reason or other
he wanted to get at you. He met Lenantais and put
paid to him. And Lenantais tried to warn you. He
appealed to me because he was a little bit less daft
than you are: he'd followed my career and knew I was
OK and would go on being OK with anyone else who
was decent . . . But I think he was wrong about you.
Don't think I come to you as an enemy, though. I
couldn't care less about what you may or may not have

done. But there *is* something *I* have to do. Lenantais appealed to me. He was murdered. And I'm going to unmask his murderer, with or without your help.'

'We can't help you,' said Baurénot. 'What you've just been saying is all Greek to us.' He smiled. 'How much of it do you really believe yourself?'

'Not all that much,' I admitted. 'But it'll do as a basis for discussion.'

'The time for discussion is over, if you ask me. Just think for a moment. We're all friends here and even if we had done what you accuse us of, I wouldn't bother beating about the bush. There's the statute of limitations for a start. What have I – what have we to be afraid of?'

'The statute of limitations doesn't apply where murder's concerned. But even if there hadn't been any murder, any sort of scandal now would reveal the sources of your present wealth, and both your comfortable little lives would go up in smoke. And if—'

'If, if!' jeered Baudrénot. 'I prefer to stick to realities. You'd better get going now, Burma . . . Phew, what a day! I shan't forget it in a hurry . . .'

He stood up. He was throwing me out!

I stood up too. There wasn't any more to be got out of him. But I meant to have the last word.

'I don't expect you will forget today,' I said. 'And nor will Deslandes . . . What was it he hurried here for? – oh yes, to tell you about his indigestion. And what was it that caused it? Oh yes – oysters . . . Unless perhaps it was a few bullets that were lying heavy on his stomach – not to mention the stomach of the cop that bought them . . . Oh well, I'll be getting along now, my friends . . . After all, there's no reason why you should trust me – Lenantais did, but he was an idealist, and I gather you two jettisoned your ideals a long time ago. Cheerio, then . . . And keep your fingers crossed in case I get run over or knocked on the head by a brick falling from a scaffolding. If I did I might be tempted to think you had something to do with it.'

I went and had a drink in the bistro in the avenue des Gobelins to wash away the taste of the Judases' champagne. Then I tried to phone my flat. No answer. Perhaps I'd dialled a wrong number. I tried again, concentrating on getting it right, but again the phone at the other end seemed to ring into an ominous silence . . .

I forgot all about Lenantais, the pont de Tolbiac, and ex-anarchists whether innocent or guilty. Rushing out of the bar, I hailed a taxi and told the driver to get me home as fast as he could.

'Belita!' I called as I opened the door.

But no one answered. I looked in the study, the bedroom, the kitchen, then in the bedroom again. They were all empty. Back in the kitchen I poured myself a drink, but forgot all about it before I'd even tasted it. I tried the bedroom once more, and this time noticed a slip of paper on the bed. On it was written, in the rather stylish hand I'd noticed on the envelope containing Lenantais's message: 'It's best I should go. S. has shown what he's capable of. He'll kill you if we stay together. I don't want that.'

You don't want him to kill *me*, my love? – but what about *you* . . . ? I laughed bitterly as I thought about

Deslandes and his oysters. I hadn't eaten any oysters either, but I could feel a horrible weight forming inside me . . . I went back into the kitchen and dispatched my drink. As I passed by a mirror I caught sight of someone wearing a very nasty expression. A very nasty expression indeed.

It was a nasty neighbourhood. I could feel it sticking to the soles of my shoes like birdlime. I seemed doomed to haunt those streets for ever in search of something – a scrap of bread, a roof over my head, a bit of love. Now I was looking for Belita. But it wasn't certain she'd come back here. In fact it was very likely she'd gone somewhere else. But *I* was here, anyway – perhaps not so much to try to find her as to settle old scores with the place. My eyes kept playing tricks on me. Whenever I caught sight of a woman she seemed to be wearing a red skirt. Perhaps that's what they mean by 'seeing red'.

I went to the Passage des Hautes-Formes, but there was nothing there. I went to where the shanty town had been at Ivry, where she'd said her people were camping, but there was nothing there. Salvador, Dolores and the rest had skedaddled, as I'd predicted. A local urchin told me he'd seen some gipsies living in an old house in the impasse du Gaz, but when I went to investigate, there was nothing there either. I went back to the camp site to check again, with the same result as before. My nerves, at least, were starting to benefit from my fatigue: a few more miles of trekking about and I might be able to sleep. I turned from the Quai d'Ivry on to the boulevard Masséna and went down past the Compressed Air Company as far the ring railway station. There was no fog today. You might almost describe the evening as cheerful. It would soon be dark, but the last rays of a yellow sun were still putting up a good fight. When I reached the intersection of the rues Cantagrel, Watt and Chevaleret, the Salvation Army building brought back the memory of Belita more intensely than ever. I imagined her as I'd last seen her that morning, charmingly dishevelled in a pair of my pyjamas . . .

'Benoit did have some dealings with the Salvation Army lately. They have some workshops there where they teach down-and-outs to mend furniture, and he sold them some bits and pieces . . .'

'And they quarrelled over the price, or over religion, and they knifed him. . . .'

'All right, make fun of me,' she said sadly. *'You do think I'm stupid!'*

'Of course I don't, darling . . .'

Darling . . . I felt as if wherever she was now she would know by a kind of telepathy that I was following up her suggestion, and would be pleased.

I went into the main Salvation Army building, where a grey-haired female in uniform redirected me to the workshop further down the street. Yes, said the angel-faced young man I found there, he remembered the elderly second-hand dealer from the Passage des Hautes-Formes . . . He'd brought some furniture . . . showed off some ugly tattoo marks . . . didn't seem a bad sort of chap, though . . .

My mind wandered to the charity's many good works. I thought of pictures I'd seen in the papers of ex-convicts back from tropical prisons and about to be taken under the Salvation Army's wing for rehabilitation . . .

I spun the young chap a yarn about being a writer – a serious author, not a sensation-monger – working on a book about reformed offenders. I confessed I'd used the second-hand dealer as a pretext because I knew he'd once had problems with the law, but what I was really interested in was ex-convicts trying to go straight . . .

After some reflection the young man came up with a suggestion. They'd recently taken on their staff one of these rehabilitated characters from a centre of theirs in the provinces, and he'd no doubt be glad to help me. Yves Lacorre was a very obliging sort of fellow.

He must be a terrible chap, Lacorre. His very name startled me. It seemed to startle everyone. Jean Deslandes had jumped when I mentioned it, though not for the same reasons.

'Could I see him?' I asked.

It turned out he wasn't in at the moment, but if I cared to come back that evening? . . .

And how!

Darling Belita! You see how you've helped me find Lenantais's murderer? For I was sure now that I'd got him. I could see the whole thing as plainly as if I'd been there.

Lenantais meets Lacorre at the Sally Army when he comes to flog his old sticks of furniture. And it's in the rue Watt, no farther away than you could spit, that the old rag-and-bone man gets stabbed. And Lacorre is holding the knife. Why didn't he steal the old man's wallet while he was about it? And why didn't he finish him off? Perhaps he was interrupted. These things happen. Why did they fight? Old animosity? No, there must have been some other reason. In his message to me Lenantais had talked of trying to save some friends. He must have meant Baurénot and Deslandes, and Lacorre must have been leaning on him for information about them. Lenantais refuses to give them away; Lacorre, in a rage, attacks him. Lacorre must have taken part in the pont de Tolbiac job in '36, but he was put away soon afterwards for killing his girl, and the other two stuck to his share of the swag; so he wants to square things up with them. Better late than never . . . When I mentioned his name in Baurénot's office, just after saying how Lenantais had been attacked by some unknown enemy, Deslandes was thrown because he immediately identified that enemy with Lacorre. Baurénot had hastily told the *crime passionel* story to cover up Deslandes's reaction.

If there were any flaws in my theory, I looked forward to getting them out of Lacorre himself that evening, and if necessary I was ready to ditch plenty of my principles in the process. So did I really have any right to criticize Baurénot and Deslandes? No, we were all the same. That wasn't the least of my regrets.

I called up Marc Covet at the *Crépu*, and began by thanking him for his article.

'Did it produce the goods?' he asked.

'Depends what you mean by goods,' I said. 'The reason I'm ringing is that it's too late to go to the National Library and I want to have a look at the papers for 1936–7. Could you get them out of your archives for me?'

'You're in luck. We've just got them up to look into the old pont de Tolbiac affair. You wouldn't be interested in that too by any chance?'

'No. It's just that I saw a piece about the death of ex-Inspector Ballin. Has anything new come up?'

'No, we're just looking for some picturesque background. The customers love mysteries . . . But come to think of it – are you sure there isn't some connection between the article you asked me to write and the murder of the cop?'

'Don't go racking your brains. The only link is that both things happened in the same arrondissement. The unity of place, you know.'

All I could dig out at the newspaper office was a report of Yves Lacorre being sentenced to twelve years' hard at a court in the provinces, at the time of the Popular Front. That was all. So in order not to have gone out of my way for nothing I looked up the case of the mysterious disappearance, on or around the pont de Tolbiac (the 'pont de Tolbiac mystery' made a good headline), of Monsieur Daniel, employee of the Cold Storage Company. I didn't find much. Monsieur Daniel was divorced and lived alone. In January 1937, and once or twice after that, his wife was supposed to have received a line or two from her ex-husband; but this seemed rather dubious. The letters were posted in Spain.

Marc Covet, hoping to wheedle the lowdown out of me, asked me to have dinner with him, but I wasn't very talkative. I was thinking about Belita. Everything

I was doing was for her, I kept telling myself, to keep my spirits up. Then I suddenly realized I'd have to move fast if I didn't want to miss Lacorre. I took a taxi to the rue Cantagrel.

It was almost ten o'clock. The fog had taken the night off, but a nasty cold wind made a perfect substitute.

The young Salvation Army man told me Lacorre still wasn't there.

'Or rather, he's been and gone. He's been much in demand today – are you sure you haven't got a rival over that book of yours? I suppose such things happen when you're dealing with these shady characters. You let slip a word about your subject, and someone else–'

'Someone else?'

'Yes, he had another visitor a little while ago, and they went off together.'

'Did he say when he'd be back?'

'Oh, he won't be long. We have to be strict about hours here, and the staff all try to set a good example . . .'

But I was already out in the icy street once more, heading for the rue Watt. Too late yet again, Nestor? Had they been too quick for me? Things never went right in this hellish district . . . But no, I was over-dramatizing. Whoever Lacorre had gone out with – a man or a woman, or the Salvation Army general – I had only to wait for him to come home again. Didn't he have to set a good example? . . .

An ideal night for hanging around. The biting wind would have satisfied the most demanding masochist. A shutter banging against a wall supplied a delightful descant. The whine of a locomotive rushing along above the rue Watt and under the pont de Tolbiac sounded almost like a siren's song. In the distance, beyond the old railway tracks, the light of cars sent a glow up over the boulevard Masséna. A sudden gust rattled in the bare branches, and among the débris it swept along the gutter in front of me was something dark and round. I bent down and picked it up. It was a Salvation Army cap.

Hallelujah! as they say.

The body couldn't be far away.

Cap in hand, as if I were a beggar – which I suppose I was, in a way – I went up back to the rue Chevaleret and then along the rue de Tolbiac to where the pont de Tolbiac begins. Not far from the spot where the late ex-Inspector Ballin had given us the slip the night before. But again no corpse. Lacorre had been nabbed, and there was no need to ask by whom. They'd certainly lost no time in making the necessary deductions – Lacorre, prison, Salvation Army – and managed to find him and pick him up. Perhaps rub him out . . .

I looked over at the Cold Storage depot on the other side of the old railway tracks. Poor Monsieur Daniel. He'd been written off as an accomplice in the robbing of his own employers when the chances were he'd been dead for twenty years. But what part had Lenantais played in the story? Murder wasn't his line at all. And he wouldn't have called me in to protect the other two against Lacorre if he'd thought they were implicated in a killing. Perhaps he didn't know about it. Perhaps the others, unable for some reason to conceal their plot itself from him, had left him in the dark about the upshot, and out of the division of the spoils. And it was because Baurénot felt guilty about this that he'd tried to help him. Human beings are like that. Neither all good nor all bad. And Lenantais, rather than tell Lacorre where he could find his old partners in crime, let himself be stabbed. They were all responsible for the death of the rag-and-bone man, the only one whose hands were clean.

Well, bye-bye, Lacorre. You've gone to join Lenantais, Monsieur Daniel and ex-Inspector Ballin. I'd have thought you were more fly, more on the ball, less trusting. You mean to say they just said come and you came, without taking any precautions?

I went back to the Salvation Army. It was only a ghost of a chance, but worth a try. My angelic young man gaped when I showed him the cap.

'It's Lacorre's, isn't it?' I said. 'Something must have happened to him. It wasn't just the wind that blew this off his head. Now listen . . . I don't suppose your people want any scandal? . . . No, well, I'm afraid there's one in the offing if you don't let me handle things my way. I'd like to cast an eye over Lacorre's possessions . . .'

'I'll have to ask . . .'

'No, no, no . . . we have to keep it quiet. Let me be frank with you . . .'

No one can resist when I'm frank with them. Angel-Face showed me where Lacorre kept his things, and among some papers arranged so that they'd come to light at once if anything happened to him, I found what I was looking for. The envelope was addressed to the local superintendent of police.

Its contents – after Yves Lacorre had given his name, date and place of birth, etc. – read as follows:

'In December 1936 I, together with two accomplices (Camille Bernis and Jean the Deserter, whom I'd met in anarchist circles), lured Monsieur Daniel, an employee of the Cold Storage Company, into an ambush. The case caused a stir at the time. I heard about some of the repercussions when I was in prison. Monsieur Daniel isn't far from his former workplace. He's in his own home. He used to live alone in a little house in the rue Brunesseau, in Ivry. He's still there, buried in the cellar. We didn't think anyone would look there. Bernis and Jean let me down, but I'll get them for it. Or they'll get me. If it's the latter, you will read this letter and proceed according to the law. The same thing if I die in my bed like anyone else, of flu or whatever.

'After we'd done the job, but before we'd divided the spoils, I trusted my accomplices enough to go away for a bit to see my girlfriend in Morlaix, where I'd sent her to be out of the way. I trusted her too. She didn't know anything about the job, but when she found out she thought it was too dangerous and wanted to leave me. I didn't want her to give me away, so I killed her. But when I was caught I said I did it out of jealousy . . . Because this time I *was* caught – it wasn't such a well-planned job as the pont de Tolbiac business. I was unlucky, and got twelve years. That was when Bernis and Jean let me down. Anyway, I did my time, and when I came out I lay low in the provinces and didn't manage to get back to Paris until recently. I tried to find the other two, but they'd disappeared. I went and had a look at

Monsieur Daniel's house. It's still there, but empty and falling to pieces. I found out someone had bought it, but I couldn't risk asking too many questions. I expect the other two bought it with my share of the swag. As soon as I can trace the purchaser I can act . . .

'A couple of other arnarchists knew about our scheme – a man called Rochat and a counterfeiter called Lenantais. Rochat's dead. I think Lenantais is still alive. He was a fool, who thought you can make omelettes without breaking eggs. Because we needed his advice setting the job up, we kidded him there wouldn't be any bloodshed – he was against that. But anyhow he wouldn't take part in the job itself because he thought law-breaking was too risky and we'd get caught sooner or later. I wonder what he thought when the police couldn't solve the case. He was a shoemaker by trade . . .'

And Lacorre went on to describe him, including the tattoo marks.

'So there you are, superintendent. If, when you see this, I've died from natural causes, you may or may not still be looking for Bernis and Jean in connection with the pont de Tolbiac case. But if you're reading these lines because I was thrown in the river or met with some other violent end, then Bernis and Jean will be the ones who did it.'

Below the signature was a set of fingerprints. There was also a postscript, written more recently and in a different ink.

'You needn't bother about Lenantais. I found him by accident. He's a rag-and-bone man, sells old furniture, and goes by the name of Benoit. I asked him for information to help me find Bernis and Jean. We started to argue and I stabbed him. I was doing the world a favour. He was an idealist. A danger to society.'

I put this missive back in the envelope and was about to pocket it when Angel-Face, who'd been reading over my shoulder, laid a restraining hand on my arm.

'This is a police matter, monsieur,' he said.

'What about the scandal?'

He raised his eyes to heaven.

'We shall just have to take our chance.'

'If you insist, then. But just wait a day or two before you make Lacorre's last will and testament public.'

'I'll have to ask . . .'

I thrust the letter at him to quench the speech he was about to deliver. He put it back among Lacorre's things and came with me to the door.

Outside, everything slept. And Monsieur Daniel was sleeping too, over there on the other side of the boulevard Masséna, in his little house in Ivry. I don't remember how I got there – perhaps the wind, which was stronger now, blew me there – but I soon found myself leaning on the parapet of the pont National, peering through the dark to see if I could make out Monsieur Daniel's place. Through the howling of the wind I could just hear the sound of the machinery pounding away non-stop in the Compressed Air Company. A distant clock struck a few times. I shook off my reverie, filled a pipe, and went to try to light it half-way down the steps leading on to the quai d'Ivry. The rue Brunesseau was a turning on the right. I'd noticed it that afternoon during my rovings in search of Belita and the gipsies. There were buildings along one side of the street; on the other was a big patch of waste land and a sports stadium in course of construction. The buildings consisted mostly of workshops and factories of various sizes, and I walked up and down the street in both directions before I found, set back in a neglected garden, something that might at a pinch be described as a house. If the wind got any stronger it would probably blow the place down.

A chain dangled from one of the posts flanking the front gate. The feeble sound it made when I pulled it was swept away by the gale. A dog woke up nearby and started to bark. I rang again. No answer. The dog wasn't barking now. It was howling. The wall wasn't very high. I scrambled over into the garden and made for the house. Its appearance would have put off the toughest squatter. A ramp led down to the cellar. I went down the ramp, came to a door, and started to fiddle the lock. What with the wind shrieking in the leafless branches of a single gnarled old tree, the dog howling, and the musty smell issuing from inside the cellar, I felt like Nosferatu the Vampire. The lock yielded. I stepped forward and lit a match. Right. I still didn't know if there was a stiff underneath the earthen floor, but there was certainly one on top of it. A nice fresh corpse in a Sally Army uniform. Plugged full of lead. Lacorre, to judge from what I remembered of his ugly mug.

12 From the viaduc d'Austerlitz to the pont de Tolbiac

It was two o'clock in the afternoon. I was lying on my bed. Since two in the morning, when I'd got back home, I'd been living with Lenantais: seeing him, hearing him, watching him with other people. What a farce! They'd made him believe the pont de Tolbiac job had passed off quite peacefully. And to think I'd believed it myself for a little while! But Lenantais must have believed it until he died. Lacorre, when he met him, didn't undeceive him – he only asked for information about Bernis and Jean. And Lenantais, who'd never liked or trusted Lacorre, had died rather than bring trouble or danger on a couple of swine who weren't fit to tie his bootlaces. But I didn't fancy their chances now. They'd been in too much of a hurry to get rid of Lacorre. The police would soon have his letter, and it wouldn't take them long to put two and two together.

It was three o'clock by now. I'd been living with Lenantais for thirteen hours. Bernis and Jean hadn't much rope left. And I, with a word, could either hasten their fall – or warn them. A strange choice. They'd tricked Lenantais and he was dead because of it. They didn't deserve such a sacrifice. It was four o'clock now. Night was creeping on, and dense fog was gradually invading the city.

I looked up Baurénot's firm in the phone book and dialled the number. The secretary said her boss had gone to the port at Austerlitz to inspect some machinery a freighter had just delivered from England.

Two black-hulled freighters were berthed in the port at Austerlitz, their outlines blurred by the fog. A cable from an invisible crane plummeted into the hold of one of them. On the other side of the river, emerging like a round eye from a mass of roofs and tall brick chimneys, you could see – dimly, as if it suffered from a cataract – the clock of the gare de Lyon.

I made my way past the line of pillars beside the water until I came on a group of men engaged in a lively discussion. Charles Baurénot was one of them. When he saw me approaching he gave a forced smile and walked over to join me.

'Well?' he asked.

'Couldn't we go and talk somewhere quieter?' I said. 'Preferably away from the river.'

'What?'

'This way.'

After skirting round some enormous packing cases and jumping down off a landing platform, we found ourselves in the gallery running below and parallel to the quai d'Austerlitz. The only light came from a few weak bulbs high up in the ceiling.

'What the hell do you want?' growled Baurénot. 'It's all your fault, damn you!'

'What is?'

'Nothing!'

'Do you mean the peppering of Lacorre?'

'You know about that, do you, you bastard? . . . Well, it's all your fault! Deslandes lost his head . . . So where are your pals?'

'All dead, as far as I can see.'

'I meant the cops . . . Didn't you bring them with you?'

'No – but they'll be after you soon enough. Lacorre left a letter behind that spills the beans.'

'The swine!'

'It's you who's the swine!' And I told him just what I thought of him. Then:

'But I came here to give you one last chance. Now you know about Lacorre's letter you'd better make yourself scarce. But anyhow the game's up and you won't go far.'

'But you will, you bastard!' he yelled. His voice echoed among the girders like a gong.

A revolver appeared in his hand. He fired. I dived. The bullet sent my hat flying. People started shouting and gathering round. Only the sailors didn't seem to bother. Bremen, Hamburg – they'd seen it all before. I shoved aside some idiot from the Customs, got out my own revolver and charged after Baurénot, who'd made off in the direction of the quai d'Austerlitz. When I emerged from the gallery into the open he'd disappeared. The people on the quai were going about their business, showing no sign of any disturbance. I glanced around. There was nowhere for him to hide, and the fog wasn't particularly dense.

It was his hat that gave him away. The elegant trilby fell at my feet. And, looking up, I saw him climbing up one of the iron piers of the viaduct that carries the Métro across the river. Every so often he used the ornamental stonework to get a foothold, and by now he'd almost reached the level of the tracks. He'd obviously meant just to cling to the girders and hide, then come down and vanish in another direction after I'd run past, not dreaming of looking for him in such an unlikely place. But then he'd lost his hat . . .

'Pack it in!' I shouted. 'Come down and—'

I was interrupted by a shot. The bystanders who'd gathered to watch promptly melted away. I was suddenly carried away with desperation and rage. Everything was falling apart. Let it all go to hell once and for all! I threw off my overcoat, pocketed my gun, and started to swarm up the girders after Baurénot. Just as I reached the level of the Métro tracks a train thundered by. The lights from the carriages swept over me; the draught nearly blew me off my perch. I could see Baurénot running along the other track now, a tiny figure soon swallowed up by the fog. Then came a terrible cry, like the howl of a soul in torment, followed by the sound of a train approaching from the other direction. I had started out along that track too, and could feel the bridge vibrating under my feet. A fierce-eyed monster was bearing down on me. I flung myself to one side and with the energy of despair managed to hoist myself on to the balustrade at the side of the viaduct. I'd have had a marvellous view down the female passengers' blouses if they were cut low enough, and if I'd had the heart to take advantage of my position. As it was, the icy blast from the train's passing numbed my fingers as they clung to the damp metal. I lost both my grip and my foothold and took a dive into the Seine.

I came to in what I soon recognized as a river-police recovery ward. As soon as he saw me open my eyes, Florimond Faroux pounced on me.

'Not dead yet then, eh, Burma?' he said.

'Yes, I am . . . All sorts of things inside me are dead.'

'Anyway, you ought to be very grateful to the river police!'

'I'll buy them a yacht for Christmas.'

'Chuck him back in the river!' said Faroux.

He explained that he'd come along as soon as he heard about my acrobatics.

'I wanted to see you about a number of things I've discovered lately,' he said.

'I'm sure!' I answered. 'The Sally Army chap couldn't wait to tell you about Lacorre's letter, and you went to the empty house and found Lacorre's body and Monsieur Daniel's bones. And now you have to find Camille Bernis and Jean the Deserter, Lacorre's accomplices in the pont de Tolbiac affair. No problem with Bernis. He was the one I was practising my circus turn with on the Austerlitz viaduct . . .'

'Yes, we've collected the body.'

'That's something . . . But you may have more trouble with the other one. He goes by another name now, and I can't remember what it is for the moment . . . Perhaps one day . . . It depends . . .'

'He calls himself Jean Deslandes. We caught him at Ivry, burying Lacorre's body beside Daniel's bones.'

'Hell . . . But perhaps it's just as well.'

'Anyhow you're free to speak now. You can fill me in on the details. There may still be some things I don't know.'

'Don't understand, you mean . . . All right, I'll try to explain.'

Which I did, but without mentioning Inspector Ballin. He was a bargaining counter I wanted to use elsewhere.

'Well,' he said when I'd finished, 'so the Lenantais-Benoit affair *was* just an ordinary mugging!'

'I never said that!'

'Talking of muggings, I don't quite understand what happened to Norbert Ballin. Was that an ordinary mugging too, or were Lacorre and Co. involved?'

'I don't think so. Ballin's death just seems to have thrown a scare into them. Made them lose their heads and start making fatal mistakes.'

'Rather a strange coincidence, though, don't you think? . . . I don't like to speak ill of poor old Ballin, but he wasn't very bright . . . If only it had occurred to him – not at first perhaps, but after devoting his whole life to the case – if only it had occurred to him to look into the matter of Daniel's house, who bought it and so on . . .'

'Well, it *didn't* occur to him,' I said. 'Any more than it occurred to him that there might be an anarchist aspect to the affair. Still, if he'd lived a bit longer . . .'

'That's right. Insult his memory.'

But I wasn't insulting his memory. The idea of an anarchist crime had merely struck the ex-inspector rather late in the day, and at a bad moment too. Bad for him, that is. Covet's article attracted his attention, and he'd have known through the local cops that Lenantais hoarded press cuttings. So he decided to go and have a look – just when Salvador was hunting for someone in a sheepskin jacket so that he could make a button-hole in the back of it. But after all it was Ballin's death that had triggered off the dénouement. In a way he'd solved his case posthumously. Not every cop can say as much.

'If ever we find out who shot him we'll show him what's what!' said Faroux.

'I should hope so!'

'I'll leave you now – you're getting delirious again! Feeling sympathetic towards cops!'

Twenty-four hours later I was on my feet again. But I hadn't yet finished with the 13th arrondissement. I set out to look for Belita, Salvador and Dolores. I imagined what I'd say to Salvador.

'Listen, Salvador,' I'd say. 'You just give Belita some peace, drop some of your racial prejudices, and swear a solemn oath to leave us both alone in future – and I don't know you killed Inspector Norbert Ballin! But if by any chance you try any of your old tricks again, I turn you in and you really get it in the neck for the murder. A cop's a cop, even when he's retired, and the cops are famous for their team spirit.'

That's what I intended to suggest to Salvador. But first I had to find him. And to find Belita with him.

I went alone through the streets where we had both gone together. Where the pont de Tolbiac begins, the rue du Chevaleret passes underneath the rue de

Tolbiac, and there's a parapet just before the 62 bus stop. As I leaned over the parapet I saw her coming in my direction along the rue du Chevaleret. There was no mistaking that buoyant dancer's step, the easy swing of the hips. I could almost hear the red skirt swishing against the flat-heeled leather boots. The same studded belt; the same unruly hair; the same earrings; the same pretty face with its wilful expression; the same proud, promising and disturbing bosom.

'Belita!'

She looked up, tossing her black hair back in a familiar gesture. Then she started to run towards me, taking the rue Ulysse-Trelat, which slopes gently up to the iron bridge.

'Belita!'

I took her in my arms, held her tight and kissed her. She was only a kid. Some of her gestures were those of a child. When I kissed her she'd sometimes hang round my neck with her feet off the ground, one leg bent back as if to ward off intruders. And that's what she did that November afternoon on the pont de Tolbiac, as an express sped by with a deafening clatter on the rails below. I felt her give a start and clutch at me desperately. Her eyes rolled wildly, then were veiled in a kind of fog. Her lips still pressed to mine, she gave a little cry, and my mouth was filled with her blood. Belita! I clasped her to me with all my might, though even as I did so I could feel my strength ebbing from me. When my hand moved up her back as if in a last caress, it encountered the inlaid handle of a long flick-knife, plunged in up to the hilt.

I stood stockstill. I laid my cheek on her hair. I

looked around to find the hellhound who'd done it. He was standing down in the middle of the rue Ulysse-Trelat, his hands in the pockets of his leather jacket, smiling with satisfaction. I picked Belita up and carried her through a frightened crowd to a nearby café. Before I went in I took one last look along the rue de Tolbiac, towards the spot where the cops had found ex-Inspector Ballin stabbed to death. If you're avenged, Inspector, you owe it to a gipsy, one of the girls you probably looked down on. Can't help laughing, can you?

I went into the café with my red and black burden and laid Belita down on a leather bench. Gently, gently, as if I was afraid of waking her. Then I went over to the telephone.

Paris 1956

Other books by Léo Malet
The Rats of Montsouris £3.99

'Then, slowly, without quite knowing why, I retraced my steps. Was it because of the redhead or because of the man with the tattoo? I think on the whole, it was because of the redhead . . .'

A rendezvous with a fellow ex-POW leads Nestor Burma, dynamic chief of the Fiat Lux Detective Agency, to a dimly lit bar in the rue du Moulin-de-la-Vierge. A venue quite empty of both windmills and virgins . . .

What he finds there is his tattooed mate, now part of a gang of burglars called the Rats of Montsouris. But this particular Rat is on to something so big he can only trust Burma. And when someone betrays him, the question remains – what *are* the back streets of the 14th arrondissement hiding?

Burma, assisted by the beautiful Hélène, is in for a string of seedy surprises . . .

120 rue de la Gare £3.99

*'We'd arrived in Lyon, Lyon-Perrache station to be precise. It was
two o'clock by my watch and I had a nasty taste in my mouth . . .'*

Nestor Burma has seen a lot of strange men die in his time. So when
a soldier without a name utters the dying words '120 rue de la Gare',
the chief of the famous Fiat Lux Detective Agency is only mildly
intrigued.

It's when a colleague meets death gasping the same phrase that
Burma's interest – and fury – are fully aroused. Time to take out his
pipe, discover the secret of the morbid address and nail the murderer
in one fell swoop.

One problem. Where *is* 120 rue de la Gare?

All Pan Books are available at your local bookshop or newsagent, or can be ordered direct from the publisher. Indicate the number of copies required and fill in the form below.

Send to: Pan C. S. Dept
                Macmillan Distribution Ltd
                Houndmills Basingstoke RG21 2XS
or phone: 0256 29242, quoting title, author and Credit Card number.

Please enclose a remittance* to the value of the cover price plus £1.00 for the first book plus 50p per copy for each additional book ordered.

*Payment may be made in sterling by UK personal cheque, postal order, sterling draft or international money order, made payable to Pan Books Ltd.

Alternatively by Barclaycard/Access/Amex/Diners

Card No.

Expiry Date

_____
Signature

Applicable only in the UK and BFPO addresses.

While every effort is made to keep prices low, it is sometimes necessary to increase prices at short notice. Pan Books reserve the right to show on covers and charge new retail prices which may differ from those advertised in the text or elsewhere.

NAME AND ADDRESS IN BLOCK LETTERS PLEASE

....

Name _____

Address _____

_____

_____

_____ 3/87